To Die In Glory

To Die In Glory

Unflinching Book III

Stuart G. Yates

Also by Stuart G. Yates

- Unflinching

- In The Blood

- Varangian

- Varangian 2 (King of the Norse)

- Burnt Offerings

- Whipped Up

- Splintered Ice

- The Sandman Cometh

- Roadkill

- Tears in the Fabric of Time

Acknowledgments

A big thank you, as always, to the team at Next Chapter, and a very special mention for Alex Davis who helped me make this Western what it is.

'Conflict follows wrongdoing as surely as flies follow the herd'
Attributed to Doc Holiday, infamous gunfighter

Contents

One

Three men in long, drab dustcoats, faces obscured by the shadow of their broad-brimmed hats, rode into the town of Glory at the start of a new day, the sky iron-grey like everyone's mood. Grim. Winter bit deep, forcing townsfolk, when they braved the elements, to scurry from door to door, hunched up, swathed in thick coats, scarves, gloves and hats, memories of the long, dry summer almost forgotten. The rains, when they did finally come, brought a deluge, causing flash floods, catching ranchers unawares, inundating land, sweeping away cattle and other livestock. Soon blizzards and snow followed. Now everything from tiny field mice to the largest, strongest residents shivered and cursed behind closed doors. Except for the three men who arrived, rigid in the saddle, their eyes set straight ahead, faces hard, chiselled from granite. Or ice. Cold as the air they breathed.

Across the street Old Man Dempsey, who had seen many things in his eighty-odd years, tipped his rocking chair forward and studied the men keenly. Their demeanour seized his attention; their expressions, the way they wore their guns. Men on a mission. He watched them turn as if responding to some silent order, dismount and tie their horse reins to the hitching rail outside the Golden Nugget saloon. The lead man gave a cursory glance down one end of the street to the other before motioning to his companions. Together they mounted the steps, clumped across the raised boardwalk, spurs singing, and disappeared through the double-swing doors. Dempsey leaned over to his left and sent a trail of tobacco juice into the dirt. He scratched his armpit, grunting loudly as he stood up, and hobbled over the hard, impacted ground towards the Golden Nugget to satisfy his curiosity.

Within, the depressive mood hung thick like a cloud. At this time of day customers were few. A couple of businessmen sporting Derby hats and tweed suits ate their breakfast in the corner whilst Wilmer Bryant, the pot-boy, looking half-asleep, swept the floor with a wide broom. Lester Tomms, the bar-keeper, polished a glass before filling it with whisky then slid it over to the stranger leaning against the counter. The other two strangers were standing some distance apart, one at each end of the long bar. The leader sampled the whisky, smacked his lips in appreciation and downed the whole drink. He indicated another needed pouring and flicked his fingers to the other men. Tomms took the hint, poured out three more whiskies and went to either end with the drink. When he returned to the centre, he stood back, never allowing his eyes to settle too long on any of them. By now, the tension had developed into a palpable thing, broken momentarily when Dempsey came wandering through the doors. No one spoke.

Looking up from another round of polishing, Tomms cracked his face in a forced attempt at a smile and, relieved, beckoned for the old-timer to move closer. As Dempsey went to take his first step, the stranger in the middle threw the second whisky down and turned. He arched a single eyebrow towards Dempsey, who stopped, mouth dropping open.

"You know where the sheriff is?"

The man's voice was low, deep, bereft of emotion. Hunching his shoulders, Dempsey tried to look away but the stranger's eyes seemed to lock him up tight, with nowhere to go. He swallowed loudly, "I reckon he's in his office."

"Fetch him."

And the stranger turned again to Tomms and motioned with his glass for a refill.

Dempsey tried another swallow, but his throat was now dry. He could do with a drink himself and he gave a little jig, somewhat unconsciously, licking his lips as he tasted the imaginary shot of good whisky sliding down to simmer in his stomach.

"Best do it now, boy," said the stranger closest to him, leaning against the counter, one foot propped up on the rail running along its lower edge.

Dempsey jumped, snapped his head to the owner of the voice, tipped his hat and rushed outside.

The cold hit him like a punch, but he didn't care a fig for any of that. His rickety old legs propelled him down into the street as fast as he could manage. Something wasn't right with those boys, he felt it in his water.

Two

Out on Cemetery Hill, over-looking the town of Bovey, exposed to the elements, Simms stood in his thick coat and stared towards the graves. There were two, side by side, one so much smaller than its neighbour, rough-hewn crosses at their heads proclaiming the names and dates of demise. Caleb and Noreen Simms. Whoever carved them did not know Noreen's birth date, but the little boy's was there for all the world to see. The same day as his death. And that of his mother's too.

In a tight cluster, the other mourners, all four of them, hands clasped in front of their stomachs, looked down into those gaping holes without speaking. Reverend Tucker had spoken the words and now the only sound was that of the wind.

Martinson was the first to break the silence, slipping over to Simms's side, brushing the detective's arm lightly with his fingers. "You okay?"

Forcing himself to drag up an awareness of where he was, Simms sucked in his lips and muttered, "What do you think?"

There was no answer to such a question. Martinson's cheeks reddened somewhat and he screwed up the cap he held in his hands, not knowing what to do or say. What does anyone say at such a time? Clearing his throat, Martinson mumbled, "I'm so sorry."

"No more than me." said Simms, turning away and moving down the hillside towards the town. He settled his hat onto his head, conscious of the chill wind but not affected by it. He doubted anything would ever affect him again.

Moving through Main Street of Bovey, most people did their best to avoid his stare, some stopping to doff hats, or utter awkward-sounding words of sympathy, commiserations or whatever the hell any of them thought it best to say.

Like Martinson, they probably thought it best to say nothing at all at a time such as this. Grief. Total, all-consuming. Simms strode like a somnambulist to his office door, face blank, and stepped inside.

The tiny office, so cold, so unwelcoming, oozed with memories of yesterday and he stood in the doorway for a long time, building up the courage to venture within.

Yesterday.

He'd sat behind his desk, scribbling down the reply to the telegram the Pinkerton Headquarters in Chicago sent him. The news seemed grave and their demands, as always, short and to the point. 'Travel to Glory. Stop. Contact US Marshal travelling there. Stop. Vital you arrive as soon as possible.'

But then Wilbur Brunt came through the door at a run and his wild eyes spoke volumes. Already on his feet, a lump the size of a melon developing in his throat, Simms managed, "What's happened?"

Noreen took to her bed, on the doctor's advice, some three days ago. Old Jim Meadows said the baby had turned in her womb. "It's going to be mighty difficult, Detective. No point me saying otherwise."

"What can we do?"

"Not a lot to do. We need to wait, she needs to rest. Let nature take its course."

On the morning he left for his office, to pen his reply to the telegram, she'd smiled up at him from beneath the covers. "I'll be fine. You go, get it done. "

But she hadn't been fine. And then the message came.

He rode with Wilbur Brunt, pounding out of the town and cutting across the open range towards the little ranch he and Noreen had set up together. After putting paid to the contract killer Beaudelaire Talpas, a period of calm and peace followed. It seemed to Simms life might be taking a new turn, one free from violence and fear. As he threw himself from the saddle and burst through the door of his ranch house, Doctor Jim Meadows caught him around the waist, holding him tight. "It's too late, son. She's gone."

The baby too. She'd wanted him to be called Caleb, if it were a boy. So Caleb it was, the name engraved on the simple wooden cross marking his place. Beside his mother, Noreen. Saved from almost certain death out on the plains by Simms. But he couldn't save her this time, not from the fever, which struck her down so quickly. Meadows said it was typhus, someone else Scarletina, but Simms wasn't listening. They were dead. Who the hell cared what from?

So here he stood, on the threshold of his miserable office, his life laid waste. He eased the door closed and turned the key in the lock. In the bottom drawer of his desk was the unopened bottle of Bourbon someone from the Town Council presented him on the day of the opening of the first Pinkerton office established in the West. Not a drinking man, Simms had put it away. Sitting down with a deep sigh, he pulled open the cork stopper and, having no glass or cup, raised it to his lips and drank.

He didn't stop drinking until the bottle was empty.

Three

Old Man Dempsey was half jogging alongside the sheriff, who took enormous steps on his walk through Glory towards the saloon. He held a loaded carbine in the crook of his arm, and a holstered Colt Dragoon at his hip. He chewed tobacco but, other than that, his face remained hard and focused.

"There was three of them," rattled Dempsey, out of breath, fighting hard to keep up with the sheriff. "They seemed mean."

"You said that."

They passed Stockton's Livery Stable, with Stockton in the doorway, arms folded across his barrel chest. "You want some help there, sheriff?"

"I reckon not," came the reply, but Dempsey, panting, close to his limit, veered away from the lawman and staggered over to where the big horse-trader stood.

"I think there's gonna be trouble."

Stockton frowned, "I can see he is resolute. What has riled him so?"

"Three strangers, gunslingers I reckon. They look like avenging angels, and from the way they spoke I reckon they is on some sort of mission."

"Avenging angels? Why in the hell do you say that?"

"Just an inkling. They appear single-minded, hard. The one who spoke to me, he put the fear of God into me."

"You're old, with a tendency to exaggerate, Dempsey. The whole town knows it."

Shaking his head, Dempsey turned his eyes towards the swiftly diminishing figure of the sheriff. "There's gonna be trouble. I knows it."

Stockton grunted. "And to think I was gonna go and visit my niece today, partake of tea and cream cakes." He leaned forward, hawked and spat into the dirt. "I'll get my shotgun."

The saloon crackled with tension as the sheriff pushed open the twin swing doors and stepped inside. He met the wild eyes of the two businessmen sitting in the far corner, white as sheets, twiddling their thumbs, before taking in the men positioned along the counter. To his left stood the first, foot on the rail, grey coat pulled back to reveal the big Dragoon at his hip. In the centre, the tallest, rolling a tumbler of whisky between his palms and, over at the far end, the third, eyes locked in on the sheriff's. No one moved; the seconds ticked by.

"Dylan," said the barkeep, clearing his throat, flat up against the wall, long mirror to his back, "these gentlemen …"

The tall one chuckled, pushed the glass away and turned. He wore two guns, but the smile he wore struck Dylan as far more deadly. "Is that what they call you now?"

The sheriff frowned. "Do I know you?"

"You should."

"My name is Dylan Forbes and I'm sheriff of this town. I hear—"

"Dylan Forbes … Must have taken you a fair time to think that one up."

"Mister, I don't know who you are, but I think you should—"

"Oh, you know all right. And I know you." The smile transformed into a sneer. "Thing is, when last we met, you went by the name of Lance. Lance Sinclair."

The air froze. Everything froze. No one breathed. Dylan felt his stomach turn, becoming liquid, horrible, sickening. Fear, total, gripped him, causing limbs to grow heavy and useless. He struggled to remain steady on legs which no longer had the strength to support him. A low moan escaped from his lips.

"I see it's all coming back to you, Lance."

Stepping away from the counter, the man at the far end crossed to the businessmen and laid his hand on the shoulder of the closest, whose eyes, like those of a puppy dog, looked up. "Please," he said, voice a whimper.

"You're both witnesses to this."

The sheriff forced a swallow, shooting his glance from the tall one to the one to his left. "I …"

"Sure you remember. Of course you do, Lance." A smile, as slick as an eel, spread ever wider across his face. "You knew this day would come."

"No, no, I never …"

"Sure you did."

"Your Day of Judgement," said the one to his left.

The sheriff shot him a look and watched the way the man's hand drifted closer to the butt of his revolver.

Dylan moved, swinging up the carbine, but the tall man was faster and the two bullets from his revolver hit the sheriff in the chest, throwing him back out into the street with the force of their impact.

The nearest businessman let out a whine and the barkeep slid down the wall, face in hands, whimpering like a small child.

"Do shut him up," said the killer, stepping towards the doors. The one at the end leaned across the counter and put two bullets into Tomms's chest. The whining stopped.

"Oh God Almighty," wailed the businessman, knocking away the third stranger's hand from his shoulder. He stood up with such a violent jerk he sent his chair backwards to the floor. "You murdering bastards!"

"Oh shit …" The stranger beside him put his own revolver to the smaller businessman's head and blew the back of his skull off, sending a shower of blood and brains behind him.

The second businessman turned white and collapsed in a dead faint, next to his murdered friend.

"Well, at least we can have some quiet now," and the stranger caught the amused expression of the one by the door just as Dylan's killer went outside into the sunlight.

Coming around the corner at a run, Stockton ground to a halt as he watched the sheriff's body come blasting out through the doors to land on his back in the street, arms thrown out, blood pumping from the two holes close to his heart. "Oh sweet Jesus," Stockton moaned, moving forward towards the stricken lawman as if in a dream. He pulled up again as the swing doors opened and a tall stranger in a long grey coat stepped out onto the boardwalk, a smoking revolver in his fist.

Their eyes met.

Stockton, not remembering he held a twin-barrelled shotgun in his hand, whirled around and made as if to run. He didn't make the first step.

The tall stranger shot him with a well-aimed shot in the back of his head.

Then, a short while later, the three strangers put a rope around the dead sheriff's neck and hanged him from a telegraph post just off the main street of the small, rundown town of Glory.

Four

A small crowd of gaggling townsfolk gathered outside the closed office, some peering through the glass, most moving away after a few moments, disinterested. When Martinson came, he did not hesitate. Pushing those closest aside, he snapped his foot against the door several times, kicking it in, almost falling flat on his face when he eventually broke through.

A jumble of voices, curious but unconcerned, looking for gossip, not wishing to offer any assistance. "Where is he?" asked someone. "Is he hurt? Is he dead?" On his knees in the doorway, Martinson climbed to his feet, dusted off his trousers and rounded on them.

"I'll take it from here," he said.

"I heard a gunshot."

Martinson, not liking the sound of that, ushered them away, returned the door to an upright position and, before wedging it into the door well, smiled a distinct 'goodbye' to the onlookers.

In the corner, behind his desk, Simms lay slumped in a heap, a trail of vomit drooling from the corner of his mouth, the empty whisky bottle rolling backwards and forwards next to his gun. Getting down on his haunches, Martinson checked the body. There was no sign of blood and he let out a long sigh before setting about making a pot of coffee.

Sometime later, Simms sat hunched up in his swivel chair, chin on chest, moaning low like a wounded bear. Across the other side of the desk, Martinson absently clicked the Navy Colt's cylinder from one empty chamber to the next. He stared at the top of Simms's slumped head. "What were you hoping to do, blow your brains out?"

"Something like that."

"I'm glad you failed."

"I was blind drunk." Slowly, Simms brought his head up, his face chalk-white, eyes red-rimmed. "Maybe when I'm sobered up my aim will be back to what it was."

"You can get that thought out of your head straight away."

"Why the fuck should I."

Shaking his head, Martinson leaned on the desk, clenching his teeth, "This isn't like you. Caving in, giving up. You've been through so much, Simms. Give it time."

"Why didn't you come for me when she took bad?" Martinson leaned back, mouth opening slightly, the anger leaving him, replaced by uncertainty, even dread. Simms stared at his friend through bloodshot eyes. "That's the part I don't understand, why you sent for Doc Meadows, but not me."

"Hell, Simms, everything happened so quick I – I was sitting with her, like you asked me, and it came on so sudden like. I didn't know what to do for the best. She had been coughing, coughing all morning, but it got worse. So bad it doubled her up, made her face as red as blood. She started screaming, telling me the baby was coming. I ran out and got hold of Wilbur, told him to fetch you whilst I went for Meadows. There's no complexity to it, just me trying to do the best I could."

"Well, I suppose, but even so." He grew silent for a moment, eyes staring into nothingness and his voice much lower and more distant. "Meadows, he said there was nothing to do, but I would give anything to have been with her. At the end, I mean."

"Yes. Yes, I know."

"There's no reason in any of it. I knew she was ill, but … For the boy to dic, an infant."

"Meadows said it was the stress, her being so ill and all."

"I thought it was a head cold, nothing more. She seemed fine, and she still had a month to go before the baby came, so Meadows said."

"You can't blame yourself. It's life, Simms. All of us, we could all do things differently, better, if we had the chance. But we can't. We can't bring it back."

"I've sat out on that prairie many a long year and wondered why things happen the way they do and I can't reach no answers. I have sat in holes in the ground, stinking in my own shit and piss, as scared as hell, wishing to die quick and easy, but I never did. I came through it all. Through that ghastly war, and lately through my time with the Pinkertons. I have hunted cold-blooded killers and put them in the ground, without conscience. They deserved to die. But that little boy – what did he ever do to harm anyone? Answer me that."

"There ain't no point in looking for someone to blame for the simple reason there is no one to blame."

"'cepting God, whatever the hell He is."

"Fate brought you and Noreen together, and fate tore you apart. You could call that God, I guess."

"I don't know anything about any of that, Martinson. We're just blades of grass. We die, and the rest just keeps on growing, as if we'd never been there at all. I look at people, living their lives, and no one stops to consider what happened to me, Noreen or the child."

"That's because they have their own lives. You can't blame them for that."

"No, I don't blame them. I don't blame anyone. It's just all such a heap of shit, Martinson. I got through so many life and death events and I'm wondering what the hell it was all for."

"You're a survivor."

"You reckon? Well, I'm not sure I'm gonna survive this."

"You will. Time. Time will be your helper, Simms. It'll not make you forget, but it will ease the pain. I lost my own wife to scarlet fever, as you know, and there ain't a day passes by that I don't think of her. I loved her, and I love her still. But I don't cry no more. At least, not as much."

"Well, it's a mystery, is what you're saying. Love. Perhaps love is God, in a strange kind of way. I don't know. I don't know much about anything anymore. I guess I'll continue doing what I do, but – I remember after the War ended and we was disbanded, I made my way down to Louisiana and the great city of New Orleans. My, that was some place. I got me to talking with someone who told me they had heard some music composed by a German guy by the name of Back, or Bark, somesuch name. He said it was the most wonderful thing he'd ever heard, brought him as close to God as he could imagine. Anyway, the strange thing is, an orchestra had sailed across the ocean from Europe to play this man's music. Imagine that, to sail across the ocean! Dear God. Well, I went along to hear and, you can guess what I'm about to say – it *was* God's music. I came out of that theatre as if in a dream and I stayed that way for a long time. "

"So what happened to change your mind?"

"Time. It works both ways, Martinson. It softens the heart, eases the pain, and brings forth changes. I shot two men in a ramshackle place down in Texas and when the Rangers came, I shot them too."

"Jesus."

"I rode north and didn't stop until it was all just a distant memory. So, you see, God came and spoke to me in that music, but I didn't pay no attention to what He said. And now, I think I'm paying the price."

"You believe that? That you're being punished?"

"I reckon. And what's more, I think the dues have yet to be fully paid."

Five

"You gonna eat that piece of ham, or can I have it?"

Stella, sitting on the big man's knee, was eyeing his almost-finished dinner plate with the look of someone close to starvation. "If you must."

Not waiting for a second prompt, Stella swept up the knife and fork and set about demolishing the ham with gusto. The big man laughed and crept his fingers up her spine. She giggled and spluttered, mouth full of food. "You'll give me indigestion."

"That's not all I'm planning on giving you."

She coughed and laughed but carried on eating, taking a scrap of bread to mop up the last of the grease on the plate. As she crammed it into her mouth, the swing doors opened and the second of the three strangers stood there, disdainfully. "Clifton, Shelby wants you outside right now. He's addressing the townsfolk."

"Clifton?" Stella swivelled on his knee. "Is that your name?"

Nodding, he stood up and she almost toppled over. If she were angry, she didn't show it, choosing to cackle instead. She stood with her hands on her broad hips and cocked her head. "That's a nice name. You gonna be nice to me?"

He winked, taking up his gun belt from around the back of the chair and fastening it around his waist. Studying her with an appreciative look, he took in her full figure encased in white petticoat and red and black dress, the bodice open at the top to reveal her plump, milk white breasts. "I'm gonna be *real* nice."

"Clifton, move your sorry ass!"

Grinning, Clifton went to step past her, but she moved in front of him, barring his way, and grabbed his crotch. Her eyes grew wide. "My, you *are* a prize worth having, Clifton."

He leaned into her and kissed her full on the mouth, then eased her to one side and clumped across the saloon floor to the main entrance. He gave his companion a cold look. "Don't talk to me that way in front of others, Josh, or I'll kick *your* sorry ass all the way down the street."

Josh paled, forced down a swallow and stepped to one side. He shot Stella a glance of absolute venom, which she returned with a kiss, blown to him from her palm. As the two men batted open the swing doors and went outside, she flopped down in her chair and licked her lips. Not for the first time, she wondered who would make the best lover and who, more to the point, would pay her the most. Pickings had been few in Glory for longer than she cared to remember, but perhaps things were about to pick up. She smiled at the prospect.

* * *

Glory's glory days were far behind it. Ten years or more before, the California gold rush took grip and prospectors moved through in their thousands as the town grew from a ramshackle collection of tents and shacks to what it now was. A main street, with two saloons, a hotel, haberdashery, merchant stores, livery stables, blacksmiths, even a milliners. There were two churches, both with healthy congregations. The town thrived and people liked it so much many of them stayed. When the gold petered out and rumours circulated of silver in the mountains close by, the town had something of a revival. But now, with the silver lode growing thin, people saw little reason to stay. Someone said that within a few years, the railroad would come, but no one really took that seriously. Why would anyone want to come here?

Taking his time, Shelby stood on a chuck-wagon, its canvas cover thrown back, allowing him a good view of the crowd gathering before him. He gripped his hat two-handed across his midriff, his hair slicked down with grease, his moustache neatly combed. With his dark long-tailed coat, grey waistcoat and dark grey pinstriped trousers, he looked for all the world like a preacher or politician of some sort. Every person in that gathering, however, knew this man was responsible for the death of Sheriff Forbes. The two ivory-handled Remingtons at his hip underlined the fact. This man was a killer, and a very adept one at that.

"I'm not here to eulogise or make false promises," he began, his voice loud and confident above the murmuring of the people. They fell silent, as one, as he continued, "Nor am I here to apologise for what happened to your late, departed sheriff. I will not give the details, but he was not the man you believed him to be. His death was long overdue."

"If that's so, why did you not send him to trial?"

A few turned to this new speaker, a small, rotund gentleman with a bowler set at a jaunty angle upon his head.

"I defended myself against him, sir. I had no option but to kill him."

"And Tomms, Stockton? What about them?"

"Tomms was killed by the sheriff," explained Shelby patiently, "and the other, whom I assume is this man called Stockton, was in cahoots with Forbes. He deserved the same fate."

"So you set yourself as judge and jury?" The round gentleman cast his eyes around those close by, many of whom were nodding in agreement. "I think we should send for a Marshal to sort all of this out."

Murmurings grew louder, voices now more confident, less frightened. The round gentleman seemed to be infusing them all with a newfound sense of courage.

"What is your name, sir?"

"Prentice Lomax. I am an alderman of this town and I own the Northern-Cross Livery stable, together with The Royal Queen saloon."

"Then you are something of a town dignitary."

"You might say that."

"Then it is a wonder to me you are not mayor."

Someone close to the back piped up at the mention of this, "Mr Howard is our mayor, sir. Unfortunately, he is ill at this present time, but we are all hoping for a swift recovery."

"I see." Shelby replaced his hat and stuck his thumbs in his belt, his eyes focusing on Lomax. "Well, Mr Lomax, here is my proposal for you. You can bring together a small council of the just and good of this town to meet with me in your own Royal Queen saloon, where I shall outline my plans for this here town. Everything will be explained there, to your satisfaction."

"Why not tell us now?" said another. "Why call us all here if not to tell us what it is you are proposing?"

"Well, that was my intention, but I see I must go some way in convincing the good Mr Lomax here. So," he clapped his hands together and rubbed them briskly. "Shall we say one o'clock. That should give you time to assemble a fair council."

"I think you should tell us all what the hell is going on here," cried out a man over to the right, the small woman at his side paling, looking up into his face in alarm.

Shelby sniggered, "Well, of course, friend." He grinned. "We're taking over this here town, as from right now."

With that, he jumped down and strode off to the saloon.

Six

Simms rode out of town later that day in an attempt to clear is head. Inside, his stomach gurgled and rumbled as the many gallons of coffee he'd drunk slopped around. Forced to stop at one point, he screwed his face up before vomiting violently on the ground. He slithered down from the saddle, stumbled over to a small outcrop of rock and repeated evacuating his guts until his throat burned and the sweat rolled down his face. Gasping, he sat down, face in hands, giving himself time to recover.

The late afternoon sun was weak, the temperature already falling, and he broke into a prolonged bout of shivering. Pulling the collar of his thick coat around him, he waited, wishing he was somewhere else, wishing he could start again, go back, do everything differently. Would any of it have saved Noreen? When he first met her, a fragile, withered little thing, molested and abused by a group of Indians, he never guessed how things would develop. But develop they did. Over the months they grew close and he opened himself up to her. She listened, without ever pressing him and he knew, in the end, she would know everything about him. Because he trusted her. Because he loved her.

And now she was dead.

A shadow fell over him and he jumped back, groping for his gun. Lost in his thoughts, he did not hear the approach of the Indian until he stood there. Encased in buckskin, his black eyes glared out from the weather-beaten flesh of his face, hair hanging in two thick ropes on either side, nose flat, the lips creased into a grin.

"You are far from home, my friend."

Simms, more out of relief perhaps than joy at seeing his good friend Deep Water again, whooped with joy and embraced the scout, hugging him close, burying his face in the man's chest. "It's good to see you," said the detective.

"You look sick, my friend. Sick of the heart."

"I suppose I am. I'll tell you about it."

They rode across the plain, following an old trail into the mountains and a secluded valley, with a small stream running through the middle, trees clinging to the hillsides, a solid looking timber-framed cabin built into the side of the mountain.

Deep Water's home.

Inside, a fire roared, two chairs on either side. On the stove a pot gently bubbled and, upon an impressive looking table, the evidence of a recent hunt; skin stripped from a deer's body to dry, sinews laid out across the length of the wooden surface.

"You seemed well settled," commented Simms, sitting down with a sigh in front of the fire.

"Best take your coat off, my friend. Once outside again, the cold will eat into your very heart."

"I suppose," said Simms, unbuttoning his overcoat and draping it across the back of his chair. He put his hat on the floor beside him and leaned back, closing his eyes in contentment.

Deep Water pushed a tin cup of steaming coffee into the detective's hand. "You taught me to like this concoction," he said, settling himself down opposite his friend.

"Well, that about evens things up. You taught me a good deal too."

They smiled at each other and sipped their drinks in silence.

The fire snapped and popped, great hunks of wood glowing red and orange and, after a while, Deep Water threw two more logs into the grate and watched them ignite.

"I know of your loss," said the Indian without turning his head. "I waited for you to come, to sit, think." He sat back in his chair, face ruddy in the glow of the fire.

"I had to get away from town, my office."

"I understand. Sometimes, the need to be alone is the only thing that matters."

"Some have been kind. Martinson, of course. But most, they seem more interested in knowing *why*. Fear, I guess."

"She had a fever. A bad time, so heavy with child."

"We live in a hard world. We're never prepared for the dangers it holds."

"Except when we are out on the range. That is our world, my friend. Not kicking our heels in some dank office."

"That's true enough." Simms stretched out his legs, wiggling his toes inside his calf length boots. "If I don't get an assignment soon, I think I'll go mad."

"Are we not mad already, the both of us?"

"Could be." He smiled then almost immediately grew serious once more. "And you? How have you been?"

Deep Water shrugged. "My life lacks focus now. After Talpas breathed his last, I had time to reflect. I came to realise that I had not set my mind upon anything else. Tracking him for so long, seeking vengeance for what he did to my family, nothing else seemed important. Now – now, I have a great emptiness inside and I try and fill my days with hunting, ranging over the prairie, but not thinking too much."

"That can be dangerous, thinking."

"Yes. But I have noticed things, my friend. I have seen wagon trains, settler families, moving deeper into the West. And war-parties, some preying on the innocent. Soldiers too, riding backwards and forwards across the plain. Often, in the night, I hear the sound of distant gunfire. The struggle for control of this land has only just begun. Better to stay away, bar the door, not wander too far from the heat of a fire."

"You sound like a settler yourself. I never thought I'd meet an Indian who lives in a cabin and drinks coffee." He chuckled and stared into the bottom of his cup. "The more the Territories open up, the more the dangers will increase. Law and order are fragile things way out here, which is why the Agency has established my office in Bovey, the first of its kind. My belief is I am going to be overly busy these next few years. I could do with a good scout, whenever the need arises."

Deep Water nodded, remaining quiet. He threw the dregs of his coffee into the fire, leaned across and took Simms's own cup and repeated the action. He went over to the stove and filled up the cups.

Simms studied his friend's broad back, waiting for a response, not wishing to force the issue. Both these men owed much to the other. Without the scout's help, Simms would never have succeeded in tracking down the train robbers Lol and Chato, ridding the land of those cruel, merciless killers. Latterly, Deep

Water would not now be alive if Simms had not shot dead the sharpshooter Talpas, the man responsible for killing Deep Water's family. In his estimation, their debts were well-balanced, but what he now asked of the scout may well prove difficult to accept. So the detective waited and the seconds ticked by.

At last Deep Water turned, a steaming cup of coffee in each fist. "Would it mean me having to live closer to town?"

"No. Whenever I needed you, I'd send you a message. Perhaps even come out here myself."

"Like now."

"I don't need your services for now, my friend. I didn't even know you were living out here. If you hadn't come across me ..."

"I have been waiting for you, like I said."

"Yes. And I'm grateful. Being here, in the warm, drinking your good coffee ... Who'd have guessed it?"

"Fate brought us together, my friend. And living here is safe, *comfortable*."

"Since when have you ever wanted to be safe and comfortable?"

Stepping closer, Deep Water handed Simms his coffee and sat down. "You know me too well."

"Then you'll do it? You'll help me, when circumstances demand?"

"Do I have a choice?"

"Of course. The choice is yours, and always shall be."

"So, I will be your deputy?"

"The Agency pay me a small retainer. Any bounties accrued, they turn a blind eye to. I shall give those to you."

"I do not need money, my friend."

Simms nodded and drank his coffee.

"Stay here tonight," said the scout. "The weather will close in as the sun sinks." He stood up, stretching his limbs, returned to the stove and put down his cup. As he padded across to the door, he dipped down to his right, picked up the carbine propped against the wall and checked it. "I shall stable your horse with mine." He turned and grinned, "It is the least I can do, now that we are working together."

Seven

As he sat drumming his fingers on the tabletop, Shelby regarded each of the hastily assembled town council in turn. Most of his attention centred on the handsome features of a middle-aged woman who sat straight-backed, bonnet set askew on her plaited golden hair, her green eyes wide, mouth full-lipped, just asking to be kissed. She caught his stare and, when he didn't look away, the colour rose to her cheeks and he chuckled, "Well, thanks to you all for coming so quickly."

"We did not really have a choice," said Alderman Lomax, the closest to Shelby, indignation edging every word.

"One of your roughnecks burst into my home," said the woman.

"Certain measures had to be taken to get you all here as quickly as possible, Mrs …?"

"If it is any concern of yours, it is Hubert. What your men did was intolerable – my husband is not long dead, Mister-whoever-you-are, and you have no right to—"

"I have every right, Mrs Hubert," cut in Shelby, raising a hand, palm outwards, to prevent any further protests. "I told you, this is my town now. I do what I like."

"This is intolerable," said the third man at the table. "You can't simply ride in here and do as you damn well please."

"And you are?"

"Norton Springer. I used to own the Springer Mine Company before it closed, but I have invested much in this town, sir, and I do not see by what authority you—"

"By this authority," said Shelby, pulling out from under his coat a Smith and Wesson Model 1 revolver, which he laid down on the table with extreme care. His forefinger ran across the cylinder with an almost loving appreciation. "This little beauty holds seven bullets, enough for me to put each and every one of you in your graves without pausing for a breath."

An audible gasp reverberated around the close confines of the room.

"You are a callous, barbarous individual, and no gentleman," said Mrs Hubert, the only one of the gathering with the courage to speak out.

Shelby gave her an admiring glance. "And you, madam, are excessively pleasing on the eye."

In a sudden burst of movement she sprang to her feet, shoving her chair back, scraping the legs across the bare wooden floor. "I'll not stay and listen to your surly tone a moment longer. What you did to Sheriff Forbes was an outrage. If you expect me to sit here and listen to your—"

"Madam, beautiful though you are, your voice irritates me considerably when your temper is raised. So sit down and pipe down."

"How dare you sir," spluttered Lomax, finding his voice at last. "If it weren't for that gun of yours, and those other two brutes, I'd run you out of town myself."

"Would you, by God?"

"Yes, I would. And, I'll tell you something else, if you do not desist in your—"

In a blur, Shelby swept up his revolver and aimed it directly towards Lomax's midriff, easing back the hammer to give emphasis to his intention. "Shut the fuck up, you pompous ass. And you," he gestured towards Mrs Hubert, "sit down before I knock you down."

"You are an ignorant brute," she hissed.

"Yeah, but my guessing is you wouldn't like it any other way."

"Dear God, sir," said the fourth man at the far end, "have you no shame?"

"Shame? Sweet Jesus, if you are not the worst bunch of imperious, contemptuous, holier-than-thou ingrates I've ever come across, then I don't know who is. Now shut up and listen." He waved for Mrs Hubert to sit, which she did, biting down any further protests. Her eyes, however, blazed with fury.

"You have more fight in you than any of these other sorry bastards," said Shelby, easing off the hammer of his revolver and leaning back in his chair. "I like that. But, for now, let me concentrate on the matter-in-hand – why you are here. As I said to you, this town is now under my control. Your job is to maintain the peace, to convince any who might take it upon themselves to question or even confront either myself or my two colleagues. We do not wish to kill anyone, but we shall if needs be."

"Like you killed Sheriff Forbes."

Shelby stared directly towards Mrs Hubert. "Let me tell you about Sheriff Forbes. First and foremost, that was not his real name. He was a man called Sinclair, Lance Sinclair. Any of you heard of that name?" He waited, casting his gaze over each one. Nothing registered on any of their faces. "He arrived in Laramie about two years ago, having travelled across from New York, looking to escape justice there after he'd shot and killed a small time merchant whose wife he was knocking off."

"Dear God," said Lomax, shooting a glance towards the woman next to him, "please remember whose company you are in – your language is coarse and vulgar."

"So is your paunch, but I don't remark on it." Shelby noticed a slight flicker of amusement at the corners of Mrs Hubert's mouth, but he did not embarrass her by dwelling upon it. "Anyways, he made his way west and fell in with a gang of thieves led by a most resourceful man by the name of Cecile Hinton. Have you heard of *him*?"

The man at the end leaned forward, "I do believe I have."

"Ah, at last!" Shelby gave a half-smile, "And who are you, friend?"

"I am Marcus Jones, manager of the town bank."

"The bank which I own," interjected Springer.

"Ah," said Shelby, eyes widening in understanding. "I see. So, that is why you come to know of Hinton."

"I seem to recall receiving a telegram from Laramie," continued Jones, interlacing his fingers. "Something about a series of bank robberies. This Cecile Hinton appears to have been the connecting factor."

"Indeed he was. He and his gang accumulated quite a tidy sum, thanks to his forward planning and leadership. Hinton was a good judge of character, choosing his men wisely. And he was fair too, always distributing the takings evenly and without prejudice."

"*Takings?*" said Lomax, aghast. "Is that what you call them?"

"Poor people's money," said Mrs Hubert, "Life savings, inheritances, *stolen* without any thought or care for the suffering such acts might bring."

"Oh, now don't bleat none," said Shelby. "Perhaps you should ask your dear friend the bank manager here what happens when money is taken in a robbery."

"What does that mean," asked Lomax, looking to Jones and back again. "What are you getting at?"

"It's a new thing," said Shelby, enjoying the confusion of his guests, "something which has made its ways from Europe over to here. Started out in the East, which is no doubt where Sinclair first heard of it, and is now creeping into banks and businesses across the New Territories. You'd know all about it, of course, wouldn't you Mr Jones? Mr Springer?"

Jones remained pale-faced and silent. Mrs Hubert cleared her throat, "What is he talking about, Marcus?"

"Insurance," spat Springer. "Banks are insured, usually with companies in the big cities. They pay out varying amounts in case of theft or fire. In order to receive a payment, which might alleviate the losses incurred through such eventualities, the bank must pay a hefty premium each month."

"I see," said Mrs Hubert. "So, if I understand it, these agreements will reimburse those customers who have lost their savings?"

"That's the idea," said Shelby. "Thing is banks tend to inflate the amounts stolen."

"Not my bank, sir," said Jones, face reddening. "Such practices may occur in other establishments, but not mine."

"Well, that's mighty upstanding of you, but I couldn't give a good God damn what you do. Thing is, Sinclair, he double-crossed old Hinton and the others. He shot them all dead out in the Territory one night last summer, and made off with all their money. Bought himself a nice little spread, some cattle, settled down. Then he made himself known to the local community, ran a merchant's store, employed three or four people, joined the church – you get the picture. He became an upstanding member of the community. And then, when the previous sheriff retired and headed back east, dear God-fearing Lance Sinclair got himself elected as sheriff. Of course, by then, he'd changed his name." He smiled at each of the others around the table, noting their rigid faces, their looks of genuine despair. "He became Dylan Forbes."

"Dear God," mumbled Lomax.

"This is just a heap of nonsense," said Springer.

"No, it ain't," said Shelby. "I can show you the wanted poster with his face on it if you wish."

"Yes," said Mrs Hubert. "Yes, I'd like to see it."

Grunting, Shelby dipped inside his coat and produced a well-creased, dog-eared piece of paper, which he unfolded and smoothed out in front of him. Satisfied, he pushed it across to the woman. She studied it for a long time, before pulling up her face to hold Shelby's gaze. Her eyes grew wet. "I never knew," she said, her voice small, close to breaking.

"Let me see that," snapped Springer, jumping to his feet. He strode around the table and grabbed the poster. He stood and read, his breathing growing tremulous. "Dear God." He snapped his arm out to Lomax, who also took the paper. Soon his face too crumpled. A man at the far end who, up until now, sat in silence, looked up and mumbled something. Lomax went over and gave him the poster.

"This is Forbes all right," he said. His eyes settled on Shelby. "I'm the mayor."

"You look like hell."

The mayor shrugged, "I feel it. This," he waved the poster, "doesn't make me feel much better."

"It shouldn't make any of you feel better," said Shelby. "The truth is, you were all taken in by him. No shame in that. He took old Hinton for a ride too. That, believe you me, is not an easy thing to do."

"So," said Springer, slowly making his way back to his seat, "you tracked him down, confronted him and shot him dead."

"Yes I did. It has taken me the best part of a year to do it, moving from one shit-pile of a town to another, always asking, always looking, but never finding. Not until now."

"But . . . " Mrs Hubert shook her head, licking her bottom lip, deep in thought, "there's something I don't understand. How do you know all this, if this *Sinclair* killed Hinton and his gang? Who told you?"

"Because he didn't kill them all, Mrs Hubert. One man managed to drag himself away, to recover from the bullet wound which almost blew out his brains." Holding her gaze, he slowly pulled off his hat to reveal the thin, black scar trailing across the right side of his head. "That man was me."

Eight

In the morning Simms bade farewell to his friend, agreeing to meet up in a few days' time. He spurred his horse and set off across the open prairie, avoiding the trail, which cut through the landscape like a serpent, winding its way inexorably towards the West. However, as he came to a rise, he noted a single chuck wagon rolling across the plains with two outriders on either flank. He reined in and studied them for a moment, wondering if they were aware of the constant threat from Ute Indians in these parts. So, taking his horse carefully down to level ground, he approached the travellers, or pilgrims as many called them, keeping his hands in the open where anyone could see them.

At fifty or so paces, the wagon stopped and the outriders wheeled around. Simms spotted the woman in the driver's seat, the young boy next to her cradling a twin-barrelled shotgun. From out of the rear of the wagon emerged an older man, dressed in well-creased white shirt and green corduroy trousers. The riders moved forward at a steady pace, cautious, carbines in their laps. Simms reined in and waited.

"Can we help you, mister?" asked the first of the riders as they came up alongside Simms, who sat smiling, hands raised slightly. The men must have noticed the guns at Simms's waist, as they grew tense, eyes focusing in on the big Colt Dragoon at the detective's hip and the Navy under his right armpit. One of the men leaned forward in his saddle, bringing his carbine around to point directly towards the Pinkerton.

"Hold on," said Simms easily, "My name is Simms, Detective Simms from out of Bovey."

"Bovey? Never heard of it."

"It's a small mining town a half day's ride from here. I was returning from visiting a friend when I noticed you moving down the trail."

From behind the two riders, now standing outside of the wagon, the old man lifted his voice and said, "Bring him on over, Curly. Real careful like."

The one called Curly twitched his carbine, motioning Sims to continue forward. "As Mr Lamont says, *real* careful."

Flicking his reins, Simms did as bid. At half a dozen paces from Lamont, Curly barked, "That's far enough," and everyone came to a halt.

The old man folded his arms and considered Simms for a long time, chewing at his lip, seemingly indecisive. Simms cleared his throat, "I was travelling across the heights over yonder," he twisted in his saddle to point over to the rise. Immediately Curly brought up the carbine and aimed it directly towards the detective. Simms held his breath, tensing, his eyes holding the others. "You might want to be a little less edgy with that rifle, mister. Those things have a tendency to go off unexpectedly."

"You might just want to tell us who the hell you are and what you want here."

Simms allowed his breath to trickle out. "I've just told you who I am. I'm a detective, stationed at Bovey. What I want is simply to make sure you folks know where you're heading – this area is notorious for Utes."

"If you are who you say you are," piped up Lamont, "where's your badge of office?"

The old man's voice held a curious twang, one that Simms did not recognise. "We don't wear badges. We're not government officers, mister. Not yet, anyways."

"A detective you said? What sort of detective?"

"Pinkerton."

"That's bullshit," spat Curly, never lowering his gun. "I've heard of you. You're that outfit from out of Chicago. You have no jurisdiction out here. I served as a deputy in Leavenworth so I know what I'm talking about."

"Well, times move on," said Simms, slowly turning again, his hands outstretched and away from his sides. "I was instructed to search for the kidnappers of an old general from the War, an assignment which brought me way out here."

"War? What war?"

"Mexican War. I served under this general back in forty-seven. That's why I got the assignment. I know this territory so I was the obvious choice."

"And you decided to stay?" piped up Lamont.

"That I did. And now I'm here to tell you how you have to be mighty careful. This trail follows the old Indian route to the North West, and many a prospector has followed it hoping to find a pot of gold at the end. What they found was if they tangle with Utes, they end up dead."

Lamont nodded his gnarled head. "Will you stay for coffee? I'd like to talk some more, if you don't mind, Detective."

"Pa, are you sure—"

Lamont snapped his head towards the second rider who, up to that point, had remained quiet. "Yes I am, Lester. Now, you ride up onto that rise from where the detective came and keep watch. Curly, you stay here."

Lowering his rifle slightly, Curly gave a grunt whilst Lester, without another word, spurred his horse and galloped across the plain to the area indicated by his father.

The flaps at the back of the wagon opened and two young women stepped out. They studied Simms for some moments before dropping down to the ground. Without a word they gathered together several metal utensils and prepared the coffee. Simms dismounted and tied his horse to the rear of the wagon, nodding across to Curly, sitting astride his own horse, the rifle still there. "Relax, Curly," said Simms, "I'm one of the good guys."

Within a short while, a camp was set, the smell of coffee wafting across to where Simms sat, one of the women laying down a blanket for him. Lamont sat on an old stool, which he'd brought out of the chuck wagon, and Curly stood close by, eyes never wandering far from the detective. The others milled about, but it was the young boy, whose shotgun was now propped up against a wagon wheel, who sprung up the conversation first by asking, "Why do you carry so many guns, mister?"

Simms chuckled, but he was the only one who found any alacrity in the boy's words. Indeed the opposite was closer to what everyone else felt, as their demeanour, dour and serious, never faltered. Six pairs of eyes bore into him, expectant. Simms shifted uncomfortably on the blanket. "Tools of my trade, son."

"You ever use 'em?"

Simms stopped himself from sniggering. "Well, not much point having them if I ain't prepared to use them."

"Ever killed anyone?"

Lamont held up his hand before Simms could respond, "I think that's enough now, Tommy. You go and rustle up some feed for old Rosie and May." He grinned towards Simms. "The wagon horses."

Tommy mumbled something, moving away without a backward glance. Curly watched him before turning again towards Simms. "We have to be wary, mister. We've heard things."

"Bad things," added Lamont. "My brother and his family crossed here maybe three or four years ago. Lost his wife's sister and his youngest to fever, and his wife's father fell into a ravine and broke his neck. Against all these odds, my brother made it to California, set himself up in the meat trade and now owns a flourishing business. He sent for us last summer. That's where we're heading."

"California? That's a helluva way."

"He made it, so shall we. Up till now, thank the Lord, we've had no setbacks."

"We're blessed," said the older woman, whom Simms recognised as the one driving the wagon when he first spotted them. At this distance, Simms saw how strikingly beautiful she was. She moved over and rested her hand on Lamont's shoulder. "We're good Christian folk, mister. We have the protection of the good Lord to help get us across this prairie."

Smiling, chest beefed up with pride, Lamont looked up into the woman's face and patted her hand. "Amen to that, Annabelle. Amen to that."

"You folks Mormons, or some such?"

They all laughed at that, but not an amusing laugh. Cynical, contemptuous. "We're Christians," said Lamont, his voice taking on a serious edge, "and we hold no truck with any *new* or convoluted beliefs other than those based on the Good Book. We are Methodists. I myself am from Cornwall, in England. I settled here some twenty odd years ago, in Kansas City. But, like you said Detective, times change. We've decided to move out West to join my brother and seek our fortune before I'm too old not to bother."

One of the young women came over from the nearby fire and handed Simms a steaming cup of coffee. She stepped back, wiping her hands on her apron and smiling down at the detective. "I have to apologise if we seem somewhat abrasive in our manner, mister. The stories my father alluded to have taught us to be overly cautious."

Raising his coffee, Simms smiled back. "Not at all, miss, I fully understand." He sipped his drink, allowing the coffee to warm him, causing his eyes to close unconsciously. "That's mighty good, miss. Thank you."

She gave a little curtsey and moved back to the campfire where she busied herself pouring coffee for the others.

"That's my daughter Tabatha," explained Lamont. "Curly here is her fiancé."

"So, you've all decided to come out here together."

"We thought it for the best." Lamont looked up again at Annabelle, who remained standing at his side. "My wife, my son Lester scouting over yonder, my other daughter Angel, helping Tabatha with the coffee, and her son Tommy."

"He's the cheeky one, asking you all them questions," said Annabelle.

"He seems bright enough," said Simms, slowly drinking his coffee. "But – if you don't mind my saying so, Mr Lamont, if you have taken heed of the stories you've heard, why have you chosen this trail? The Platte might have been the wiser choice."

"We meditated on the choice long and hard, Detective. Time is pressing. My brother has acquired for us a house with an adjacent business."

"A ladies outfitters," said Annabelle, unable to contain her enthusiasm. Her face glowed with anticipation and joy. "We have such plans, Detective, such hopes for a bright and secure future. Once Tabatha and Curly are married, we shall expand, introduce new lines. San Francisco is a splendid place in which to live."

"San Francisco? So …" Simms stared down into his coffee cup. "I wish you all the very best, ma'am, I truly do, but – I've got to say this. Utes and Bannock People roam this area. They do not take kindly to settlers. The Bannocks have made some sort of pact with the Mormons; that was the reason I asked if you were of that faith. For some reason beyond my understanding, Mormons are safe from attack due to their friendship with the Bannocks."

"And you consider them a threat to anyone else?"

"I do. As are the Utes, Shoshone, possibly even their close cousins the Comanches, who have been known to range this far. These are dangerous times, Mr Lamont, and many Native people are suffering from the extremes of the weather. A family such as yours, travelling so openly across the plains …" He shook his head. "You have to be on your guard, night and day. No question."

"Our aim is to cross towards Denver, rest there for a while, perhaps even spend the winter close by before we resupply ourselves and continue west in the spring. We shall take stock of the situation from that point, so I am grateful for your wise council."

"And what do you do for food?"

A silence stretched out during which Simms looked from one face to the next.

"We get by," said Curly at last, but there was something in his tone, and their expressions, which was unsettling.

"What my son-in-law to be means," said Lamont, "is we are well provisioned."

"I see," said Simms. "Well, all things considered, I think Denver is a good idea, as are your thoughts on staying there for the winter. Out here on the plains is not a good place to be at any time of year, winter especially."

"But you should not worry unduly," put in Annabelle. "As I said, the good Lord is watching over us. My prayers will be that He watches over you also."

Simms pressed his lips together. "Oh, I have no room for any god in my life, ma'am," he looked across at the faces turned towards him, faces flat, unemotional. "No offence, but I'm not what anyone might call *close to God*."

"You sound bitter, Detective."

"Bitter? Well, yes ma'am, you could say that. This is a cruel, unforgiving land, ma'am, and I don't think God even knows it exists."

He noted their eyes narrowing, their backs straightening and, with Annabelle especially, mouths becoming thin lines of barely controlled fury. Growing increasingly more uncomfortable, Simms excused himself and stood up, handing back the empty coffee cup. He doffed his hat but didn't attempt to put out his hand towards Lamont. "Well, I wish you all well. Keep your eyes skinned, folks, and if you do come across any Natives, try not to give them cause to attack."

"Do they need cause?" asked Lamont, the only one now able to converse with Simms apparently. "I've heard all the stories of their barbarity, cruelty, all of that."

"If you take from them, they'll kill you. But mainly I believe all they really want is to be left alone. Just be mindful of that."

He left them then, mounting his horse and turning it away, heading towards Bovey many miles to the south east. Passing Lester, he gave a casual salute, which the young man returned by means of a small raising of the hand. Only then did Simms spur his mount into a gallop.

The pounding of his horse across the plain soothed him somewhat. Despite their reassurances of God and being blessed, the group troubled him. What troubled him most of all was the fact that a single wagon had made it so far across the open countryside without encountering danger. Most pioneers and the like travelled in trains of wagons, some numbering twenty or more individual carriages. A lone wagon was bound to attract attention from all the wrong sort of people. Without wanting to, his mind recalled Noreen, how she, alone, was set upon by a group of young bucks who molested and defiled her. Most probably, she would have lost her life if Simms had not arrived when he did. He shivered at the memory. Such thoughts put him into a deep depression, because if the same happened to Lamont and his family there would be nobody to come to their rescue.

And then, as the evening drew on, he saw the other wagons.

Nine

Riding out across the plain, Josh and Clifton set off from Glory in the early morning, well muffled in greatcoats, gloves and scarves. The stream of smoke from the chimneystack of the homestead, cutting through the cold air, acted like a beacon guiding the two men unerringly towards their destination.

A hundred paces from the lone cabin, with its adjacent lean-to where animals could shelter from the cold, they reined in their horses and sat, breathing hard. Clifton munched on a plug of tobacco, face screwed up against the fierce breeze assaulting his flesh like a thousand needles. "I want sour belly and eggs, with a gallon of coffee, inside me before I do anything else." He twisted in his saddle. "You reckon they got such things?"

"Could be," said Josh, his voice sounding distorted behind the folds of the scarf wrapped around the lower part of his face. "My stomach is rumbling like a brewing storm. Why the hell did Shelby want us out here so damned early?"

"Maybe he knows something we don't."

Josh narrowed his eyes. "What the hell does that mean?"

"It means I haven't got a clue why Shelby told us to come here, morning, noon or night. All he said to me was go and bring the woman back. Nothing more."

"Do we know if there even is a woman?"

"Well, there sure as hell is *somebody* in there."

"And this is Sinclair's place?"

"Can't be any other. Head directly west is what Shelby said. No other home-stead within a hundred miles is what he said. I reckon this has to be it."

"Just as Shelby said?"

"Just as Shelby said. If you ain't happy with any of this, Josh, maybe you should voice your concerns to Shelby when we get back."

"Yeah, you'd like that, wouldn't you? Rile Shelby enough for him to kill me, give you a greater share in the money."

"If there is any money. But no, Josh, I couldn't give a God damn whether you live or die in this here endeavour. All I do know is I am cold and hungry, so let us go and do what we have to do and get out of this goddamn cold."

Flicking his reins, Clifton moved on, Josh settling in next to him, both of them at a greatly reduced pace now, on edge, watchful. The cabin, a small, squat place with a simple veranda, appeared old and somewhat rickety, the timbers ill-fitting, gnarled and, in places, rotten. Its roof sagged dangerously in the middle. Better days were long behind it.

As they pulled up their horses and prepared to dismount, the front door creaked open, the woodwork so swollen with damp the inward passage proved difficult. From a gap of mere inches, the twin barrels of a shotgun poked out, a gruff, aged voice saying, "That's far enough."

Both men stopped, raising their hands slowly skywards. "That ain't no woman," hissed Josh from the corner of his mouth.

Clifton licked his lips and forced a smile. "We're here to talk to Lance's wife. Have we the right place, because we—"

"Who did you say?"

Josh quickly interjected, "That's Sheriff Forbes, is who we mean. This is his place, is it not?"

"It is, but he ain't here. He left for town yesterday and rarely comes out here during daylight."

The two men exchanged baffled looks. Josh cleared his throat, "We were told his wife would be here. We need to talk to her."

"His wife has gone."

A shocked silence. Clifton's voice sounded strained when he asked, "*Gone?* Gone where?"

"She took off with the boy yesterday, when Dylan went into town. Not sure why. Didn't ask."

Running a hand across his face, Clifton blew out his cheeks in despair. "Well, we need to talk to her. Where did she go?"

"I've a mind not to tell you. Go back to wherever it is you came from. I don't like the look of you two."

"That's as maybe, but we need to speak with her. Got a message from Dylan for her."

35

"For her? So, if you've seen Dylan, where is he? Why couldn't he give the message himself?"

"That's what we need to talk to his wife about," said Josh. "Look, mister, we mean no harm. Could you see yourself letting us inside, if only for a short while? It's mighty cold out here and we is hungry and would greatly appreciate it if you could—"

"I've told you what I want. Now get away from here before I open you up with both barrels."

Clifton chuckled, "That's a tad unfriendly, old fella, if I might say so."

"*Old fella?*" The owner of the voice, still hidden by the deep shadows of the cabin, sounded amused. The shotgun disappeared, replaced by a set of thin, twig like fingers curling around the door edge. A series of grunts and groans followed, and the door gradually, inch by painful inch, opened up a little more, allowing the person inside to step out through the gap.

Both men gawped.

Standing in the half-open doorway was a wizened, bent over woman of indeterminate age with the look of someone dried up from the inside, features pinched by the cold air, grey hair raked back from a deeply furrowed forehead, watery eyes peering out from under heavy brows. When she next spoke, her mouth was nothing more than a black hole, teeth long gone. "I am Violet's mother, damn your eyes. Now," she lifted the shotgun, the gun appearing enormous in her diminutive hands, "get off my property."

"Ah shit," said Clifton, exasperated, pulling out his Remington revolver and shooting her through the head.

They sat at the table in the centre of the single room, slurping up the steaming broth the old woman had set upon the well-stacked stove in the far corner. Neither spoke, all their concentration centred on eating as much as they could in as short a time as possible. After she'd crumpled in a bloody mess on the veranda, they'd dragged the old woman's body out into the dirt with little ceremony and stepped inside the warmth of the cabin. Checking the shotgun, Josh found it empty and he sniggered at that before tossing it away into the corner. Clifton ladled out the broth and here they were, swathed in steam, relaxed and, to a degree, content.

"What do we do now?" asked Josh sitting back in his chair, smacking his lips and belching loudly.

"I reckon Shelby's gonna be pissed about the wife leaving."

"If he'd told us what the hell he wanted to talk to her about, things might not have played out the way they have."

"That old woman would have still reacted the same way. Crazy old coot."

"Imagine living out your whole life, overcoming adversity and danger, to end up with your brains blown out in a God-forsaken place like this."

"How do you know she'd suffered adversity and danger? Maybe she'd lived a life of comfort and safety."

Josh arched a single eyebrow. "You reckon? With a face like that?"

Clifton laughed, lifted his bowl and licked around the inside, throwing it back down when he'd finished. "I guess not. Still don't answer your question about what we're gonna do now though, does it?"

"No, it does not," sighed Josh.

They lapsed into silence, both considering the remnants of their respective meals. Clifton took to reloading his revolver, cleaning out the single chamber he'd discharged, whilst Josh went across to the stove and pushed in a couple more pieces of wood to keep it burning. He rubbed his hands together and luxuriated in the warm glow of the flames.

"This is what I propose," said Clifton at length. "You set out further into the prairie and pick up the wife's trail. Meanwhile, I'll go back to Glory and tell Shelby what has transpired. Then I'll follow you and—"

"Pick up the wife's trail? What the fuck. I'm no goddamned tracker, Clifton! How in the hell am I supposed to know where she's going, for God's sake?"

Clifton looked across to Josh who, sitting on his haunches in front of the stove, seemed struck down by an unholy terror. "Hell's bells, Josh, all you gotta do is head due west. That ain't difficult."

"And where in the hell is west?"

"Well, it's kinda ..." Clifton waved his hand absently towards the left, "It's over that way."

"You're full of shit. I have no goddamned ideas where west is, or any other such direction come to that."

"We found this place, didn't we? Jesus, Josh, you are one moaning, useless piece of shit!"

"We found this place because Shelby told us it was the only place for miles around. And he was right. But to go off across the prairie with no idea which way I'm going, I'd have to be crazy. What if I get lost? What if I end up in Indian territory and have my eyes plucked out by them crazy bastards?"

"Listen, you brainless sonofabitch, you just head towards the sun. I know that much. The sun goes down in the west. That's your marker. You keep the sun straight ahead. She'll be going the same way."

"How in the hell do you know that? Maybe she's an Indian herself, a squaw heading back to her people. Maybe she knows which direction to take and maybe—"

"She's no squaw, you idiot! That old coot said she was her mother, for God's sake, and she was no Injun. Holy crap, Josh, you just don't wanna do what is right!"

"Well if you know so much about it, why don't you go west and I'll go back to Glory to tell Shelby what happened?"

Blowing out a tremendous blast of breath, Clifton brought his fist down hard on the tabletop. "Goddamn you, Josh! Goddamn you."

Sometime later, having loaded up his saddlebags with the remaining scraps of food from the log cabin, Clifton set off towards the west, doing as he said and keeping the sun directly ahead. Josh stood in the doorway, arms folded, and said nothing as his companion disappeared into the vastness of the open prairie. He went back inside, finished off a mug of coffee and wrapped himself in his coat. Outside, he struggled with the body of the woman, dragging it over the snow to return it to the cabin. He stood and looked at her, no longer recognisable as a once living human being, and shuddered. Then he went outside to the lean-to, brought his horse from where he'd stabled it and swung himself up into the saddle. Peering across to the silent, lonely cabin, he pressed his lips together and wondered if all of this heralded something much worse than any of them ever considered. Would he ever see Clifton again, he mused.

Pushing such thoughts aside, he headed back the way he had come, back to Glory and back to Shelby. As he rode, he rehearsed what he might say. No matter how he tried, he knew that Shelby's reaction was not one to relish.

Ten

He came across the two wagons as he rode parallel to the California Trail, which was not something he planned on doing. Something about his conversation with the group of pilgrims, led by Lamont, troubled Simms. They seemed unduly cautious towards a lone individual and their response to his voiced doubts about a god again struck him as being extreme. What concerned him more than anything, however, was the simple fact that they travelled alone. A small band, exposed to a hostile land, was not a strategy anyone back in their home of Kansas would have suggested. It was always better to travel in numbers and most did. Following this course did not always guarantee survival, for Utes in particular seemed none too concerned by the number of people they attacked. Nevertheless, there was a degree of safety in numbers. Now, looking down from the hillside towards the two wagons standing alone, horseless, he experienced a tension across the shoulders, a tingling deep in his lower groin. What he saw told him something very wrong had occurred here. Lifting out his carbine, he gently steered his horse down the incline, eyes alert, sweeping across the area ahead. Nothing moved and, the closer he got, the more his sense of caution and concern increased.

The two wagons were standing at an angle to each other, with a rectangular piece of tarpaulin stretched in the gap between them forming part of a circular defensive ring, or bivouac as he had heard it called. There were no horses and no sign of life.

Simms reined in his horse and eased himself down from the saddle. Advancing slowly, within a dozen paces he called out, "Hello there, I'm coming in. My name is Simms and I am a lawman from out of Bovey." Stopping, he sucked in a breath, scanning the land beyond the wagons for a moment. There was a bundle of clothes lying in the dirt, something he hadn't spotted earlier.

A sudden gust of wind blew out one of the flaps of the nearest wagon, causing Simms to drop to one knee, carbine ready to fire. He squinted down the barrel, held his breath and waited.

Nothing stirred.

Lowering the gun, he gave himself a moment to relax. He did not like being out here in the open with no cover. Memories of Beaudelaire Talpas, the sharpshooter, came to mind and he shivered and ran forward at a half-crouch, swerving a little from left to right, expecting a shot to ring out at any moment.

He slammed himself up against the side of the nearest wagon and knelt there, mouth open, ears straining for any sound. Again he looked across to the hillside from where he'd come to the horizon on the left, searching for the tiniest of fluctuations, a smudge, a shadow. Utes moved quick, often unseen. This was their land and they knew it well; every crevice, knoll and piece of scrub. Any number of them could be out there, lost amongst this vast ocean of dirt and rock.

His horse scratched at the ground but otherwise appeared calm. Usually a good sign, Simms thought to himself, and he crept along the side of the wagon, ever watchful, ready to bring his carbine to bear in an instant.

Chancing a look around the edge into the area covered by the tarpaulin, he snapped his head back again, processing what he had seen.

Two bodies, face down, blood spilled, soaking into the ground. The intense cold kept the flies away, but the icy blue tinge to exposed flesh told him all he needed to know. They were dead.

He moved closer, pulling aside the edge of the tarpaulin with the barrel of his gun. This close, the stench of decay was all too apparent. They'd been dead for some time. One body was that of a young girl, the other a fully-grown man. He didn't care to study their faces, but swung around and stood up to peer inside the first wagon.

There were two more corpses amongst the debris of the chuck wagon, throats slit, stomachs split, entrails oozing out like thick, grey ropes. Simms whirled away, hand over his mouth, fighting down the urge to vomit. He stood, taking in gulps of air, gazing at the second wagon, wondering what further horrors awaited. It took him some time to conjure up the courage to look inside.

The bodies, or what was left of them, lay in twisted attitudes, grotesque, bloodied manikins stripped of flesh, only their untouched heads revealing that once these were human beings. Four of them in all. A charnel house, a family massacred, but by whom?

He staggered away, bent double, no longer able to investigate further. Gagging, he fell to his knees and threw up, stomach heaving, throat burning with bile. The sound travelled across the expanse of bleakness all around. Anyone lurking out there would hear, but Simms no longer cared. He slumped down on his behind, panting, ripped away the bandana around his neck and used it to dab at his mouth.

For a long time he sat, staring into nothingness, his mind turning to events of ten years and more ago when, as a young soldier, promoted in the field, he led a troop to a seemingly empty adobe homestead. A dead donkey lay sprawled in the yard, belly bloated, the flies a thick, black, living blanket around its head. But within the building, a scene from hell itself.

A naked man sat in the corner, body streaked with trails of black, encrusted blood, hair splayed out in a wild halo, hands like claws clutching a half-chewed hunk of raw meat. The smell caused Simms and his men to reel backwards, two of them throwing up in the ground. One man, known as Menzies, stumbled against the far wall and fell backwards through a suspended sheet concealing a second, much smaller room. Within were stacked half a dozen or more bodies in various stages of decomposition, all of them stripped of flesh.

As Menzies screamed and swayed towards the exit like a drunkard, Simms took out his revolver and blew the naked man's head apart with a well-aimed bullet.

"Cannibals," screeched another recruit, a young boy barely eighteen, on his knees wheezing and crying. Other troopers staggered around, unable to believe the horrors, all of them sobbing whilst Simms stood and looked out across the scorched landscape and tried to rid his mind of the images.

He failed.

They came to haunt him many times. Such as now, with the reality hitting home. Faced with almost certain starvation, Lamont and his family had resorted to the butchering of their companions, to feast on their flesh, to save themselves from death. The naked Mexican, driven insane by what he had done, was only one of many such incidents. Simms knew of others. Now here it all was again; this time not in a war zone, but in the harsh land of the Territories.

He wondered how Annabelle Lamont faced her god with the truth of what she and her family had done, for Simms believed she and her husband were responsible. There was no other possible explanation. Everything fell into place, their awkwardness, their suspicion. Cannibalism. This must be the reason for what had occurred here, Simms decided. There were no signs of a struggle, no arrows stuck in the wagons' wooden sides, only the curious absence of the horses. Utes often attacked settlers for their horses. But Simms knew of no instances in which the Native peoples had butchered white people for food.

No, he felt certain Lamont undertook these heinous acts and, as such, he knew what his duty was.

Cannibalism, however awful, was not the sole reason for their arrest, of course, despite it defiling every base human emotion. Murder, cold-blooded, pre-meditated. Starving they may have been, but to do this, to slaughter their companions for meat ... Simms shook his head, deciding the best course would be to arrest them for murder. The slit throats bore testimony to that.

In something of a dream-like state, Simms crossed over to his horse, slipped the carbine back into its sheath and hauled himself up into the saddle. He took one last look at the cluster of wagons before turning away and riding across the prairie, heading back towards Lamont and his brood.

Eleven

They gathered in Mayor Howard's home, oil lamps dimmed, the fire crackling in the grate. Millie, the maid, served French brandy from a cut-glass decanter and the men sat and sipped their drinks, huddled around the impressively large table.

"If you can get off the telegram, Marcus, we may still be able to come out of this alive," said Howard.

"Sooner better than later," added Springer, curling his fingers around the bowl of the brandy glass.

"I'll need one of you to watch out for that murdering bastard," said Marcus Jones. "God knows what he'll do if he finds out."

"He'll kill us all," said Springer and shot a glance towards Lomax, the Alderman. "You do it, Prentice. Keep watch."

Lomax spluttered as the brandy caught the back of his throat, "Jesus, Norton, I'm no goddamned gunslinger."

"No one said anything about gunplay, Prentice. All you need do is keep a lookout. If that murdering swine Shelby appears, you let Marcus know quicker than you can spit, you hear me."

"I hear you."

"Good. You get the telegram off to Laramie, call in a Marshal, even soldiers if need be. We can't sit here and allow Shelby to ride roughshod over the whole of our town."

"But what he said about Forbes, or Sinclair, or whatever his damned name was," said Lomax, "what did he mean by all that?"

"I reckon," said Jones leaning forward, "Forbes killed them all for gold. And that gold is right here, in our town. And Shelby wants it."

"Can't be very much," put in Springer. "Forbes didn't live his life as if he was sitting on a fortune."

"Maybe he was waiting," suggested Howard.

"Waiting for what?"

Howard looked across the table towards Springer and shrugged. "Or maybe he'd spent it before he even got here."

"He had a wife and child," said Lomax.

"Not his," said Springer. "I knew that girl. Her name was Violet, a young girl from down Mexico way. She travelled up here some years ago with her mother and her then husband, or at least I assumed he was her husband. Consumption got him and he died, leaving her a widow. The child couldn't have been more than three years old."

"I never knew that," said Jones.

"There's a lot you don't know," sniggered Springer, draining his glass and smacking his lips. "I've made it my business to know everything that goes on around here. You have to, as a mine owner. Dealing with so many different people, from all walks of life, you never know what's around the next corner. So I listen, I ask, I find out."

"But you didn't know Forbes's real name was Sinclair," said Howard, breathing in the aroma of his brandy before tipping it down his throat.

"No. That I did not, and I'm sorry for it. If I'd have known, we never would have accepted him as sheriff."

"His credentials seemed perfect," said Lomax.

"Perhaps, in hindsight, a little *too* perfect," said Jones.

"Well, nothing we can do about any of that now," said Springer. "What's done is done. Now, we have to concentrate on limiting what happens next. Whatever Shelby's plans for our town are, you can bet your life they ain't good."

"We're already gambling with our lives, Norton," said Howard. "If he gets wind we've sent for a marshal …" He let his words disappear into the warm air and they all fell into silence, gazing into the bottoms of their glasses, all of them weighed down by their collective fears.

* * *

Mrs Hubert opened the front door of her modest home, her jaw dropping when she saw who her caller was.

Shelby chuckled, pulling off his hat in as close a thing to politeness as he could manage. "Afternoon, Mrs Hubert. I wondered if I might impose upon you for a moment or two."

"No, you may not. Now get off my porch before I—"

"Before you what? Call the Sheriff?" Shelby chuckled again, shaking his head. "Ma'am, you have nothing to fear from me. Indeed, the opposite may well be the case."

Mrs Hubert opened the door slightly wider and leaned against the frame, folding her arms. "What exactly does that mean?"

"Oh, you know."

"No, I don't. What is it you want, Mr Shelby?"

"You're a lonely widow, I'm the new governor of this here town. Maybe we should develop a relationship."

"Are you out of your mind?" It was her turn to chuckle and she swung around and closed the door with a slam, leaving Shelby to stand there, running his hat brim through his hands, grinning.

* * *

The tapping of the Morse machine seemed unnervingly loud in the confines of the tiny office. Jones skipped from foot to foot, desperate for the tiny message to end.

"The line has only been open for a year," said the operator, looking beneath his brows at the bank manager. "It's not one hundred percent guaranteed to get through."

"Yes, but you've sent them before, goddamn it!"

The man's eyes narrowed. "Mr Jones, you have no need to speak to me like that. I can only do what I can do. I am a slave to this system, with all its inherent problems. If the line is intact, Laramie will receive this message within the next ten minutes or so. You want to wait for the reply?"

Jones twisted and peered through the door towards the outside, where Lomax was standing, rigid like a stone. "No, no. I'll come back." He turned again to the operator. "Listen, when you get a reply, just bring it over to the bank. Would you do that?" He pushed across a dollar. "I'd appreciate it."

The operator squeezed his lips together, fingers hovering close to the coin. "All righty," he said at last, quickly taking the coin and slipping it into his waistcoat pocket. "I should be over in around twenty minutes, perhaps less."

"Thank you," beamed Jones, his relief palpable, and he went outside, squinting in the brilliant sunlight. Despite the cold, out in the open, the sun warmed the air slightly and Jones looked to the clear, blue sky and gave up a silent prayer of thanks.

His sense of relief was short-lived for, as he looked again at Lomax, he realised with a start why the man stood so stiffly. Some fifteen paces or so to the left was Shelby.

Jones's stomach tipped over, his bowels loosening and for a moment he almost fell. He tottered forward several steps, hands stretched out before him in supplication, "Shelby, Shelby, it's not what you think."

"For Christ's sake Marcus ..." began Lomax, snapping his head around in horror.

"Really?" asked Shelby, nonchalant, hands on hips, long coat pulled back, guns in their holsters. "And what might I be thinking, Mr Jones?"

Jones gaped, swung to Lomax, bleating, "I thought – I thought he—"

"Shut the fuck up, Marcus."

"No, no, please don't do that, Marcus," said Shelby, grinning. "Just tell me – what is it I'm supposed to be thinking? Here I was, taking an afternoon stroll, calling on some of my choicest friends and I see you coming out of the telegraph office, all perky like you just fucked your favourite young whore. What were you doing in there, Marcus?"

"Sending a telegram."

"*Really*? My oh my, I never would have believed that, you being in a telegram office and all. Well, well ..." He chuckled to himself, shaking his head. "Perhaps you'd like to enlighten me on just what sort of telegram you were sending. And to whom?"

"Head office," blurted Lomax quickly, before Marcus had the chance to say anything further. "There's been a run on money from the bank, you see. Marcus was simply messaging his Head Office over in Laramie, asking them for more funds."

"And advice," added Marcus.

"Yes," said Lomax enthusiastically. "Advice. We're all worried about it, you see, Shelby. Customers. The townsfolk. They're worried, what with the death of Dylan and Stockton, it's shaken them up."

Shelby stood, silent, considering their words. "So if I were to go on inside and see the typescript, that's what I'd read, yes?"

"Of course," said Lomax he grinning towards his bank manager companion. "Isn't that right, Marcus?"

"Oh yes. Yes. Absolutely."

"All right," said Shelby and he took a step, "that's exactly what I'll do."

Twelve

The gunfire came to him from across the prairie, long before he saw the reason for it. Spurring his horse, Simms broke into a gallop, heading straight as an arrow towards the sound. With his head down and teeth clenched, dismissive of the sharp cold air biting into his body, he veered slightly off the right towards a steep sided cluster of rock. Once there, he threw himself down from his horse, taking a moment to calm her. Steaming breath gushed from her flared nostrils, eyes blazing as he stroked her quivering neck. He gently tied her to a nearby tree, pulled the carbine from the sheath next to the saddle and made his way carefully over the assorted rocks and boulders.

From this vantage point he saw the drama being played out below.

Standing some way off, exposed to every element and every enemy, Lamont's chuck wagon afforded the family a degree of shelter by no means sufficient to protect them from the Utes, who circled ever closer. Simms wriggled over a large boulder, catching sight of two bodies lying festooned with arrows. Meanwhile, the two-horse team screamed in panic, lashing out with their hooves, horror-struck by the gunfire pouring out from behind and to the side of the wagon. Lamont stood, an old musket in his hands, frantically ramming home another shot whilst beside him Lester sent off a steady fusillade of fire from his revolver.

Up to that point, none of the shots seemed to have hit the Utes who, emboldened by the lack of marksmanship, moved forward, stopping every few paces to loose off another stream of arrows. The end was not far off.

Cursing, Simms eased himself forward. He was between perhaps one-hundred and fifty and two-hundred paces from the besieged wagon. He doubted the carbine could hit its mark from such a range, but even if it could, he'd need to bring his revolvers to bear in order to put down more than one Ute. He needed to get closer but dared not reveal himself. Not yet; not until he was in range with his Dragoon.

A strangulated shriek carried across the plain from the wagon and he craned his neck to see Lamont staggering backwards, clutching at an arrow imbedded in his neck. The musket slipped from his fingers and he dropped into a bizarre sitting attitude whilst Lester cried out, "Daddy, no, please, Daddy!"

Two arrows struck Lester as moved to his father's side. He teetered forward and dropped to his knees just as a Ute pounced, gripping the young man's hair to pull back his head and expose the neck. The hatchet flashed in the air and chopped through tendons and arteries, the blood spurting out in a fan-like arc as the Ute repeatedly struck home. What was left of Lester pitched into the dirt and lay motionless.

Whooping with victory, the Ute stepped over the young man's body and moved across to Lamont. But by now Simms was in range and he fired a single round from the carbine and hit the warrior between the eyes.

Not waiting to witness the results, Simms broke cover, vaulting over the remaining rocks and ran, casting the carbine aside. The remaining six or so Utes stood transfixed, not daring to believe what they saw. At that point, someone fired from within the wagon and dumped one of the Indians to the ground, a hole the size of saucepan lid in his chest.

Galvanised into action, the Utes took up a terrible battle-cry, knives and hatchets appearing from inside buckskin vests, and advanced at a trot towards the Pinkerton.

Breathless, Simms stopped and waited. He stood, controlling his breathing, counting each step the Utes took. They appeared not to notice his calmness, the way he remained still. Perhaps such a reaction was alien to them, having only ever confronted settlers or others with little experience of gunfights and killing. Well used to overcoming men and women fresh from the east, some even broke out into laughter.

Simms stood, the breeze playing around the rim of his long coat, but no other part of him moving. Totally in control, the outcome already decided.

At fifteen paces, Simms brought up his revolvers and opened up on the advancing Natives, each shot fired with measured accuracy. Lifting each revolver slightly after each discharge to clear the cylinders of powder debris, he worked methodically, patient, deliberate and, with each shot, a Ute Indian died. The heavy sound of the revolvers filled the open plain, six shots in all.

And then, in a frighteningly short span of time, there was nothing but silence. It was over.

* * *

Having checked the bodies, Simms took to cleaning out and reloading his firearms. Whilst he did so, Annabelle sat beside Lamont. She had next to her a small basin into which she dipped a neckerchief, using it to dab away at the angry looking arrow wound in the old man's neck. The arrowhead was deep but, when he came over, Simms could see it would take not much more than a strong yank to free it from the flesh. If not, the wound would fester. Within two or three days, the old man would be dead. He might die anyway, even with the damn thing extracted. Utes tended not to keep their arrowheads particularly clean, using them more than once to bring down game. Surgeons back in the War often told him they felt certain dirt had a lot to do with men dying after receiving even minor wounds in battle. No one could be certain, but it seemed to make sense. Simms had witnessed more than enough deaths to know just how dangerous untreated wounds could be.

Annabelle looked up at him, her face strained with the skirmish, the death. Tears rolled down her cheeks. "Why did you come back?"

"I think you know."

Her face creased into a frown. "You found the other wagons?"

Simms grunted, sighed and looked across to the Lamont's wagon. "How many did you lose?"

"Too many." Her voice cracked and she broke down, body racked with gut-wrenching sobs.

From out of his world of pain, Lamont spoke up, voice firm. "They killed Angela and Tommy first. We made camp, got to preparing a meal, when two of them showed up on ponies so thin you could count their ribs. They rattled out in their sinful language, indicating our horses."

"That doesn't surprise me," said Simms, shaking his head despairingly. "They'll do anything for horses."

"Which is what they did, damn them all to hell." Lamont, seized by a sudden stab of pain, convulsed and groaned, clenching his teeth. He sucked in his breath and Simms waited for the wave to pass. "I told them in no uncertain terms we would not give up our horses. That's when all hell broke loose and the others came out from the cover of the rocks, firing their arrows. Tommy went down first and …" He cut off, eyes squeezing shut, tears springing forth.

"You don't have to give me the details," said Simms. "Where is Curly?"

"He took off with Tabatha." He looked into Simms's wide-eyed expression. "I told him to, Detective. I told him to take our horses and get as far away as possible. I knew these devils would not desist until we were all dead."

"And then you came," said Annabelle, her sobs receding. "An angel of mercy."

"But too damn late," said Simms bitterly. "I'm sorry for your loss, Lamont. I truly am. But the reason I came back …" He rubbed his face, gaze moving from the old man to his wife. "What in the name of God did you do to those people?"

"What we had to," said Annabelle. "The Lord came to me, Detective, in a dream. We knew we would never make it. Food had run out. All we had was grain for the horses. And He spoke to me. At our lowest point, in the depths of despair, He came to me and told me what we had to do."

"*God* told you to kill and eat those people? Is that what you're telling me?"

"It was the only way. We had to survive."

"And how did you choose?"

Both of them looked blank, confused. "I don't understand," said Lamont.

"How did you pick who to kill and eat first," said Simms, his voice frayed, the anger almost getting the better of him. "Because you did kill them, didn't you."

"We had no choice."

"You had every choice, you sonofabitch." He stepped back, his body trembling with rage. In his hand was the reloaded Dragoon, its big barrel pointing unerringly towards the old man. "Did you feed Tommy their flesh? Did he know?"

"What do you take us for, Detective," shrieked Annabelle, hands spreading out, "We're not savages! Of course he didn't know. Nor did the girls. We kept it from them."

"So, you butchered those people, cut them up and did what – salted the meat, stored it to keep you all alive?"

"We did what we had to do," repeated Lamont, sounding as if he were reading from a script. "The Lord showed us the way. The Lord is never wrong."

"You sanctimonious bastard," spat Simms, easing back the hammer of his gun. "I'm taking you both back to Bovey, where you'll stand trial for murder."

"We can't allow you to do that," said Annabelle, sniffing loudly and climbing to her feet. "We're continuing East, Detective. It is our destiny."

"Your *destiny* is to find yourselves swinging from the end of a rope."

"No." She smiled, a warm, disarming smile which lit up her lovely face, pushing aside all the strain, all of the heartache. "What happened, happened. We have paid our dues. We have lost our children."

"And we shall meet them again," said Lamont, eyes closed, struggling to overcome the pain. "We shall all be together, in the kingdom of God."

Seized by a sudden and violent bout of coughing, Lamont rolled onto his side, knees coming to his chest, hands pawing at the arrow, blood erupting from his mouth.

"Oh sweet Jesus," cried Annabelle, flinging herself over the old man, pulling him close to her. She looked up at Simms, her eyes wide, pleading. "For pity's sake, help me get him to the wagon. I have to pull out this damn arrow."

For a moment, Simms dithered, but then he holstered his gun, making his decision. Together with Annabelle, he helped lift the old man and carried him over to the wagon. All the time he wondered how he could take them both back to Bovey without further violence.

Thirteen

On the morning of the second day, Clifton knew he was lost. The trail, if there ever was one, seemed to have vanished and he spent several unproductive and increasingly frustrating hours searching through bits of scrub for anything – a hoof print, remnants of a campfire, a piece of discarded clothing or scrap of food. But he found nothing. As the panic set in he made the decision to camp, take his bearings and head back to Glory. Due east. All he had to do was follow the sun.

But how to do that when the sun would be forever moving across the sky, *away* from where he wanted to go? Following it west proved comparatively easy; there was a point in his journey when he grew almost smug at his developing skill. East, however, was something else entirely.

A trickle of a river meandered through the endless plain. He let his horse drift over to the bank and dip its head to take a prolonged drink. He slid down from the saddle, using his hat as a form of ladle, scooping up enough water to drench his head and face with. Thirst slaked, he slumped down on the muddy side to watch the river flow slowly by. The dreadful thought that he had not seen it on his outward journey took root and dominated every thought. Where to go, what to do. His food, nothing more than a few shards of hardtack, would be expended before the day was out. The horse, munching on the tufts of coarse grass which sprang up along the river's edge, would fare far better than he ever could. He rubbed his face and whimpered.

Stretching himself out, he pulled the brim of his hat over his face and tried to rest. The cold was bearable down here beside the river. Keeping his mind away from what the night might bring, he ruminated on his options and soon realised he had none. His only course was to continue heading east. If the sky remained clear, he may have a chance, however slim. Things could become difficult, however, if cloud cover blocked out the sun. Then what would he do?

"Ah damn it," he said and sat up. He should never have agreed to Josh's arguments. Right now that bastard would be sat in the warmth of the saloon, drinking whisky and gnawing on steaks. Shelby, angry no doubt, would nevertheless have accepted the inevitable. Forbes, if he had any money, had spent the lot or secreted it away in a place unknown. Without his woman, the probability was it would remain hidden forever more.

Letting out a long sigh, Clifton gripped hold of his horse's reins and hauled himself up to his feet. He stretched, arching his back, a few joints cracking audibly. As he shook himself and went to place his foot in the stirrup, a shape moved out of the corner of his eye and he froze. With agonising slowness, he turned his head and gasped.

A woman, blue-black hair pulled back from a face of startling beauty, stood, a single-barrelled shotgun in her hands. Beside her, clinging to the hem of her dress was a small boy, all in white, shivering.

"You use your left hand to take out your pistol and you do it slowly. I know how to use this."

Clifton, struggling to breathe easily through his partly opened mouth, kept his eyes locked on hers and did precisely as she said. Holding the Remington by the butt, he lifted it from the holster.

"Take it, Leo."

Without a pause, the little boy scuttled across the space between them and snatched the revolver from Clifton's fingers. In another blink, he was standing beside the woman once more.

"Now." The woman raised the shotgun slightly to train the barrel directly towards Clifton's body, "You tell me why you have been following me for the best part of two days."

Clifton gawped and, taken completely aback by her question, tried his best to find the words which might convince her of anything but the truth.

Fourteen

Looking up from behind his desk, the telegraph operator shook his head, a genuinely apologetic expression crossing his face. "I can't break the law, mister, no matter what you say. Unless you're a lawman, I can't disclose the contents of the telegram."

"Were you at the meeting?"

The operator frowned. "Meeting? I don't think I quite understand. What mee—"

"When I stood out in the street and informed everyone that this now *my* town."

"I'm sure if I was there, I would have remembered such a thing. But, my old mother has been bad these past weeks and all of my spare time has been—"

"I ain't interested in your excuses," said Shelby, irritated by the man's obstinacy. He leaned across the desk, the Model 1 having materialised in his hand. "You show me the message or I'll decorate this office with your brains."

The street was almost empty when Shelby stepped out once more from the telegraph office. The only people standing there were Lomax and Jones, faces masks of pure terror. Regarding them with an expression of utter contempt, Shelby approached the two men, shaking his head. "To say I am disappointed is something of an understatement," he said, stopping some four paces away. "You lied to me, gentlemen."

"It's not what you think," blurted Lomax in a rush, "We merely wanted to ascertain the true nature of—"

"Don't make it any worse by telling more lies, Prentice," said Shelby. "I read the message, you idiot. Sending for a U.S. Marshal. I'm let down by your betrayal." His eyes narrowed, "From both of you."

"We sent for that marshal long before you turned up," said Lomax. "All we were doing was making sure he was coming."

"You sent for him before?" Shelby put his hands on his hips and looked sky-wards, smiling, "You sent for him because there was a dispute over mineral rights. Nothing to do with me and my boys." He slowly brought his gaze to bear on the two men again. "I'm not an idiot, so don't treat me like one. I checked and this message," he brandished the telegram, "this is something entirely different. You for sent a marshal and a team of deputies, this time to run me out. Don't deny it."

"What did you expect," said Jones, doing his utmost to remain resolute. He drew in a breath. "Whatever your argument with Dylan, you murdered him. Stockton too. You expect us to simply sit back and do nothing?"

"I expect you to do as you're told." Shelby moved closer, reaching out his right hand, clamping it over Jones's shoulder. "Marcus, as bank manager, you have access to the safe. I think I'll be making a deposit. As soon as my boys return, I'll need to place a substantial sum in your bank." Marcus's mouth set to trembling. "Before you come over all self-righteous, the money is mine – by rights. So don't go fretting none."

"Money you stole, you mean," said Lomax through clenched teeth. "Once the Marshal gets here, things will be very different, you mark my words."

"With the weather the way it is, by the time the marshal gets here, we'll be long gone. However, seeing as you're more than likely to continue on this course of betrayal you've set yourself upon—"

Lomax spluttered, "*Betrayal*? What in the name of God are you talking about? We haven't *betrayed* you, Shelby, we're protecting ourselves."

"Well …" Shelby titled his head, "Call it what you will, I'm not going to take any more chances. My only regret is I didn't do this sooner." He swung around, threw back his coat and drew the Smith and Wesson Model 1. He took a bead on the timber pole attached to the side of the telegraph office, held his breath and shot off first one then the second glass insulators placed on the crossbeam some twenty or so feet above him. The gunshots reverberated around the deserted town streets like the thunder of an approaching storm. Perhaps that was precisely what they were. For as one of the wires from the pole separated with a pronounced snap, Shelby turned, rammed the Model 1 into Lomax's guts and shot him twice.

Jones shrieked as his companion, the town Alderman, staggered backwards, clutching at the ruined remains of his abdomen, blood and mangled pieces of body tissue leaking out between his fingers. He dropped to his knees, face screwed up in abject agony.

"You murdering bastard," said Jones and went to help his dying friend. But Shelby was there first, arm stretched out like a bar to prevent Jones from taking another step.

"I'll kill every last one of you," snarled Shelby. "Nobody crosses me. Now get back to the others and you tell them what has happened here."

"But you can't leave him like *this*," pleaded Jones.

And it was true. Shelby poked his tongue out and ran the tip along his top lip as he considered Lomax, bent double, groaning and sobbing, put the gun against the ailing alderman's head and ended his life with a single bullet in the brain.

* * *

They stood in a ragged line, heads bowed save for Mrs Hubert who, head uplifted, was ramrod straight, eyes fixed and defiant. As two large men lifted Lomax's body, draped in a dull, grey sheet, and placed it in the rear of a low-loader, the undertaker, dressed in his uniform of jet-black, shuffled over to Norton Springer. "I shall prepare the body for viewing, as instructed." He then bowed his head and moved away, the driver of the low wagon flicking the reins to fall in behind him.

Mrs Hubert rounded on the others. "What are we supposed to say to his wife?"

Springer's breath trickled out from his thin mouth, "The truth, I suppose."

"That he was shot down like a dog?" Her fists came up, clenched so tight the knuckles glared white beneath the skin, "If I were a man, I'd show that murdering fiend what justice is. Damn your hide, Norton, why don't you *do* something?"

Casting a swift glance across the street towards the saloon, he swallowed hard. "And what exactly would you like me to do? Eh? Walk in there and shoot him?"

"That would be a good start, yes."

"You don't mean that, Mary. I'm not a killer."

"No, but you know people who are."

He blinked, stumbled over his words, shocked. "Mary, you can't – what the hell are you suggesting?"

Howard and Jones drew closer. Jones, trembling as if suffering from severe cold, kept his head lowered, voice tiny and afraid. "We can't do anything, Mrs Hubert. The man's an animal."

"No, no," said Howard, "Mary's right. Norton, you've employed a lot of fairly questionable characters in your mine. You must surely know some you could employ to—"

"Are you insane," said Springer. "You're suggesting we murder him?"

"It's not murder," replied Howard. "Perhaps they could just run him out of town after roughing him up a little. We have to make a stand."

"Like Prentice did?" said Jones. They all drew silent at that, the enormity of the words' meaning sinking home.

"My late husband had a gun," said Mrs Hubert after some time. "If you're not willing to do anything, Norton, then I shall."

"You'd shoot him, Mary? Are you sure you could do that?"

"What choice do we have? All you can offer is surrender! That man in there," she shot out her finger towards the saloon, "has just murdered Prentice in cold blood. We can't stand idly by and allow him to get away with it. What will he do next? Burn the town down and us along with it?"

"He wouldn't do that," said Jones, his face continuing to stare at the ground, "He told me he wanted to deposit money in the bank."

"Blood money."

"Mary's right, Norton," said Howard. "We can't let this go unpunished. He's already murdered Forbes and Stockton, and now this. It'll be days, perhaps weeks before a marshal arrives—"

"If one ever does," interjected Mrs Hubert.

"Indeed. Norton, you must know someone, surely?"

Springer closed his eyes and took several deep breaths. "There might be someone. Tobias Budd was his name, a giant of a man, something of a bare-knuckle boxer. He came in with a team of workers two years ago and worked until the mine was spent. Then he took a wife, bought a little spread a half day's ride from here with what he'd earned. I think he might still be there, although I can't be sure. Nobody can be sure in these uncertain times."

"But it's worth a shot," said Howard, unable to contain his enthusiasm. "If we were to offer him enough money, he just might ..."

They all stood, gazing at Springer with wide, expectant eyes. Even Jones, hopeful, looked out from those red-rimmed eyes of his.

"I'll ride out after dark," said Springer. "If Shelby gets wind of what we're thinking of doing …" His voice trailed away, no further explanation needed.

In the quiet of the early evening, when even the town dogs preferred to remain hidden, fearful for their lives, Mrs Hubert walked through the doors of the Golden Nugget and sought out Shelby. He sat alone in the far corner, dealing cards in a game of patience, not flickering as she stepped up to him, her patent leather shoes clinking loudly across the bar in the still air.

She sat down opposite him, her clutch bag on her lap, eyes hard and piercing. "You're an animal," she said at long last.

"I reckon we all are," he said, not taking his eyes from his game. "What do you want, Mrs Hubert? Reconsidered my offer?"

She gave a sharp laugh, "Dear God, you think mighty highly of yourself, don't you."

Shelby shrugged, snapping down a card and sitting back, contemplating her with an amused expression. "I know I said as soon as the money is in the bank we'd be leaving, but seeing you sitting here, so close, I've a mind to stay. We could be good together, you and me."

"That will never happen."

"Oh? And why not? A lonely widow such as yourself, you must be longing for someone to warm your bed. And me," he leaned forward, elbows resting on the table, "I would warm it better than most."

"You have no need of me, Mr Shelby. You have that whore – Stella. Vent all of your lusts and deprivations on her."

"I don't want a whore. I want a wife, a home. All of the things I have never had. The first moment I saw you, I knew you would be the one."

Her jaw dropped and for a moment, she did not have the ability to speak. "Sir, how could you possibly think…"

"Come now, Mrs Hubert. I'm not as bad as you believe I am."

"You shot poor Mr Lomax stone dead in the middle of Main Street. I know very well how *bad* you are, Mr Shelby."

"I did what I had to. Call it *management* if you will. I managed the situation, in order to bring about order. If there is no order, there is chaos. And chaos leads to even more killing."

"My God, I think you actually believe what you're saying. You justify the murder of an innocent man with the most meaningless of reasons. Chaos? It is *you* who has brought chaos, Mr Shelby, as soon as you and your men rode into town and murdered our sheriff. You're a wild, rabid beast and, like any such animal, you should be put down." Her hand emerged from her lap and in it was a small, pocket sized Navy Colt. She eased back the hammer.

Shelby gaped and slowly raised his hands, eyes glued on the gun. "Now, you just be real easy with that there thing, Mrs Hubert."

"I'm going to shoot you dead, just as you did Mr Lomax. No one else has the guts to do it, but I have."

"I am certain of that, but think, please. My offer to you is a sincere one. I will change. Once we have the money, we can go anywhere, do anything."

"Blood money is what it is. I'll have nothing to do with it, nor anything to do with you."

"Mrs Hubert – can I call you Mary? That's your name, is it not? Mary, please, listen to me, I have wandered off the path, but I promise you, I am good in heart. I would protect you, give you everything you ever wished for and more. We could go away somewhere, somewhere far away, start again, leave this God-awful place far behind. You and me. Think about it, please. Before you pull that trigger, think about the life you could have. With me."

His boyish smile caused her to falter. Did she recognise some glimmer of truth in his words, a sincerity she convinced herself was not part of his makeup? Her loneliness ate away at her, not that she would ever admit to such a thing. In the town of Glory, there wasn't anybody who could offer her solace, comfort, affection. Often she had considered moving away, back East, to begin again. She was still young and she was well aware of the effect she had on men, the longing in their eyes so plain to see. And now, this man, this villain, so audacious and yet so *convincing*. Perhaps he could change, perhaps he could offer her a life, a life unlike any she ever dreamed possible. Perhaps.

The gun, so heavy in her hand, brought her back to reality and, as the strength drained from her shoulders, she lowered it to the table top, a shuddering breath escaping from her lips. Very gently, Shelby reached over and took the gun from her fingers and, with his other hand, closed it around hers. "Thank you," he said.

She brought up her face and, as a single tear rolled down her cheek, she gathered her bag, turned and walked out of the saloon without a backward glance.

Fifteen

Rather than travel back to Bovey, Simms decided it best to take Annabelle to his ranch house. As he buried Lamont and the others, she stood, face blank, lips moving in silent prayers. Several hours later, with the bodies in the ground, he took an assortment of blankets from the wagon and, wrapping the woman in them, set off across the plain. They shared his horse. The sun was already low in the sky and he was mindful of how cold it would become. A snowstorm loomed in the solid, white canvas overhead.

With Annabelle pressed into his back, they managed to keep one another warm. By the time the first flakes drifted from above, they were in the valley which led to his ranch.

The cabin appeared as he'd left it, empty and lonely; its coldness, far more pronounced than even the surrounding air, oozed from every joint. He hadn't dared return, not since Noreen's death, deliberately staying away, putting images of her and the baby out of his mind. He decided to return when he felt strong enough, but circumstances, as always, contrived to create their own agenda and, powerless, here he was. He reined in the horse, sat and stared. Annabelle, who must have dozed off, sat up, stretched and yawned. "Is this your place?"

A simple one storey cabin, built with the help of Martinson and a few others, with a narrow veranda and a single, shuttered window. Deceptive. Inside its deepness became apparent, with two other rooms adjacent to the main living room and, out back, a barn and small outhouse with privy. In time, the project already started, several fields, which formed the rest of the estate, would be fenced, but at the moment only one was completed. Simms dropped down from the saddle and held out his hands to ease Annabelle to the ground also. He then took the horse to the rear, where he unsaddled it and put it into the barn. By the time he stomped back to the front, the snow was coming down hard and Annabelle stood, covered in a thin blanket of soft, white flakes.

Forced to put his shoulder against the swollen door, he stood on the threshold and stared, not knowing what he would find. The table and chairs gazed back at him, just as he'd left them; the empty fireplace, the rocking chair on one side, easy chair on the other. Across to his right, the half-open door leading to the bedroom, with the bed where Noreen…

Sighing, he crossed to the fireplace, working at clearing away the ash and soot from the grate. Barely conscious of the woman moving around behind him, he stacked up logs, stuffing the spaces in between with kindling and set it alight. Kneeling, he tended to the flickering flames, gently blowing the tiny, glowing embers, bringing the fire to life. When at last it caught, he stepped back, brushing away the soot from his trousers.

Annabelle had her back to him in the doorway, staring out into the evening, the quickly descending night lit by the snow flurries falling like a curtain all around. The silence was a living thing, pressing in upon them and he joined her, standing in silence, to watch.

"It's so beautiful," she said, voice no more than a whisper.

"Yes, it is. But let's thank God we're not out in it."

She turned to him and the closeness of her body caused him to stop and hold his breath. "We have a lot to thank God for, Detective. But most of all, for you."

He cocked his head. "Ma'am, you might not be saying that when I take you to Bovey to stand trial for what you did."

"Necessity," she said simply.

"Murder. Murder is never necessary."

"You say that as if you yourself have never killed anyone. But I know you have. I saw you shooting those Indians. You were – you were a machine. No emotion, no hesitation; a systematic, even ruthless determination to see them dead."

"I was protecting us, ma'am. You know that. They would have taken their fill of you, then scalped you and left you out in the prairie to bleed to death."

"That may have been preferable to what you have in store for me."

"Ma'am, I think what you need is a large dose of reality. Your husband stepped across the line with what he did. And you'll answer for it, as his accomplice."

"You're a hard man."

"No, I'm simply doing my duty, is all." He took her firmly by the elbow and guided her inside. He closed the door and barred it. He then took off his coat and shook it out whilst Annabelle went across to the fire and settled herself into the rocking chair. She sat in silence, gazing at the burning logs, as a picture loomed up in Simms's mind. A picture of Noreen doing the exact same thing. Pressing the back of his hand against his mouth, he suppressed a sob but no amount of effort could rid his mind of the life he had lost.

Later, he tied her ankles together and she lay, stretched out in the smaller of the two bedrooms, without struggle or complaint. Her eyes were wide open, empty, far, far away.

"If I need my toilet," she asked, voice low, as if all the fight had left her.

"Just call out and I'll accompany you." He saw something in her face, and quickly added, "Don't fret none – I'll wait outside."

"So trusting."

He clicked his tongue and went into the other bedroom. For a long time he stood and gazed down at the mattress. If he tried hard enough, he could still make out the indentation of her shape and, when he lay down, her perfume. He rolled over, did his utmost to block it out, but he failed. Sometime in the night, with the wind howling outside, he cried and sleep would not come. At first light, he climbed out from beneath the blankets and, half freezing, took to stacking up the fire once more.

Once he'd untied her legs, she struggled to and from the privy. Later, they sat at the crude table and ate some slivers of bacon. "It's all I got," he said, noting how she pulled down the corners of her mouth.

She blew out a sharp breath. "It's too salty," and she pushed the unfinished plate away and drank down her coffee. Ignoring her, he finished his own meal without further comment.

Crossing to the door, he struggled opening it and gasped as he looked out across an endless ocean of white, above and below. Groaning, he leaned against the door well and wondered what he might do.

"We're snowed in," she said, coming up beside him. "What can we do?"

"I don't know," he said. "I have little food, a few ounces of flour, some salt."

"I can use it to make bread."

They exchanged a look. "We might be here for some time."

"Then, we'll have to make the best of it."

Sixteen

A little way from the river, a small camp was set with a fire, an iron pot placed upon the flames. It bubbled and steamed and Leo stirred it with a large wooden spoon whilst the woman sat on a rock, swathed in a blanket, the shotgun in her lap. "You better tell me the whole thing, mister. My patience has all run out."

Clifton sat across from her, his arms wrapped around his chest, hands tucked under armpits, wishing he too had such a thick, warm looking blanket. The temperature continued to drop markedly and a quick glance to the sky told him all he needed to know. Gathering clouds, dense, grey and ominous, spoke of a snowstorm.

"I don't know all the details," he said, teeth chattering, "but I could sure use some of that stew."

Her eyes never flickered. "You can have some when you tell me."

Nodding, he scrunched himself up smaller still, "Your husband, he's an old friend of my partner. They had some sort of a quarrel, but I'm not sure of the details. All I know is it had something to do with money – a lot of money. When Shelby came to us with the deal, at first we thought he was—"

"Hold on, mister. *Husband*? Who in the hell is that? My husband died some three years ago now."

"He did? Well – well, who was the sheriff then? You were living with him, or so the old woman said when we—"

"That old witch? You went to Dylan's cabin, is that what you're telling me, and the old woman told you I was his wife?"

"Not exactly, she sort of – look, like I said, I don't know the details. Shelby told us to drop into your place and find out where the money is. The old woman, she came on real nasty, like she was meaning to kill us and …" He shrugged, looking away.

"So you shot her? Killed her?"

"We had no choice, she was—"

"Spare me the justifications, mister. You shot her dead. And now you're meaning to do the same with me."

"No." Clifton threw out his hands, "No, I swear that wasn't our intention! It was all a ghastly accident. We were there to find out where the money is stashed, nothing more."

"Money? I know nothing about no money."

"But – but that can't be. Forbes took the money. He and Shelby were part of a gang. They'd robbed a few banks, made themselves a pretty penny, but then Forbes double-crossed them, left them for dead. But Shelby, he's as tough as a wild bear. He recovered, brought us in on his plan to get back his money. He killed the sheriff, which I believe was a mistake; he should have found out about the money first."

"Us?" Clifton frowned at her question. "You said 'us'. There's more of you out here looking for me?"

"No, Josh went back into town to tell Shelby the money was gone. I set to following you, but – hell, you know the rest."

She shifted position and nodded towards the boy. "That'll be ready now, Leo. Put some of that stew in two bowls, one for yourself, and the other for – what did you say your name was?"

"Clifton. Clifton Brown."

She remained stoic, gesturing to the boy to do as she said. Clifton watched the boy filling up a wooden bowl with piping hot stew, chunks of vegetable and meat oozing over the side. Licking his lips, Clifton eased his hands out from under his arms. "I appreciate your kindness, ma'am."

"You ain't tasted it yet."

Smiling, he took the proffered bowl and wooden spoon and, balancing it on the rock beside him, set about slurping down great mouthfuls, holding his mouth open and sucking in the cold air, cooling down the stew to help it on its way.

The boy, returning to his own bowl, sat cross-legged close to the fire and ate in silence, his eyes never leaving Clifton. The woman remained sitting, waiting.

"Less than a year ago, Dylan arrived on our land," she said without preamble, "and we took him in and gave him hot food and coffee. He said he'd been out on the range, with his family, and they'd taken sick. He'd left them to try to find help, but on his return to the wagon found his wife and child both dead, struck down with fever. He cried as he told his story and I do not believe my heart had ever reached out so strongly towards another human being. Well, he laid himself out in the barn and in the night he came inside. My husband, Nathan, he sat up wondering what was happening and Dylan …" For the first time since he'd met her, Clifton saw her face crumple, the hard exterior giving way to the pain of loss. "Dylan killed him. Right there. Drove a knife deep into his heart, pulled him outside and dropped him to the ground. Then he came back and he…" She looked away, gathering up a corner of the blanket to wipe away the tears from her cheeks. "He stayed with us for a few days, having his way with me. You understand my meaning?" Clifton nodded, the speed with which he ate slowing down, all his attention centred on her words. "He asked me if there was a town nearby, a place where he could go. So I told him of Glory and he took me and Leo with him. We packed up a wagon, made our way to town and over the next few days he wormed his way into their trust, just as he had Nathan and me. He was a charmer, I guess is what I'm saying. His smile so warm and friendly, his demeanour so …" She sniffed loudly, face returning to its hardness. "He bought old mother Reynolds' place. Told me she was *his* mother. Another lie. All of it lies. Old Blythe Reynolds, she said she would have to stay. He liked that idea. Made his play-acting more believable. So we stayed and he had me every night whilst Leo lay in the bed in the corner, listening to him grunting and groaning." Her mouth turned down. "I thought I was in hell, that I was being punished for what I'd done. I'm half Shoshone, my mother captured by a soldier on a raid. I saw him shoot her one night in a drunken rage. I was fourteen. I took down the shotgun from its place on the wall and I killed him. Ever since then, I've been putting my past behind me, until I met Nathan. The kindest, most loving man I've ever … Leo was born six years ago and I…" In a sudden flurry of movement, she flung back the blanket and strode over to the pot sizzling on the fire. "Watch him, Leon," she said. Without a word, Leon picked up Clifton's Remington from the ground beside him and cradled it in his hands.

As she squatted and ate from another bowl, Clifton finished his and laid it gently on the rock. Wiping his mouth with the back of his hand, he said, "Why did you wait until now to leave him?"

She snapped her head up, eyes flashing. "Don't think I didn't want to. I longed for the day when I could get away. But I knew he'd follow, track me down, perhaps kill me. Leo too. I couldn't take that risk, but when he didn't come home the other night, I knew. I knew something had happened. He *always* came home, always at the same time, like clockwork. I'd sit and watch the timepiece moving around and when it chimed eight, I knew the next thing I'd hear would be his horse stomping up outside the door. Then he'd come in, demanding his supper. Old Blythe would waddle around, doing his bidding, then he'd drag me into the bed and have me. The only times he didn't was when he came home too drunk to even see straight. I longed for those times, prayed for 'em."

"So when he didn't come home, you got up and left."

"And the rest you know."

"And you too. He's dead. You're free."

"Free. You call this being free?" She chuckled and set to attacking her stew once more.

"At least you're alive. And the boy."

"For now. My aim is to make for Riverneck. It's a town another two day's ride from here. All I need do is follow the course of yonder river. But I'll be crossing Bannock land. I'll have to be careful."

"I could help you," said Clifton quickly. He paled at her furious look. "I'm good with a gun. I'll protect you."

"You couldn't even find me, you fool! We'll fare better without the protection of one such as you. You wanted to find me to kill me!"

"No, to get the money."

"There is no money – I told you that."

"I find that hard to believe. Shelby is difficult to hoodwink. Forbes had the money and he's hidden it away some place. Shelby will find it, no matter what."

"And what will he do with you?"

"He'll kill me. I failed him, and he is not a man to upset."

"So you'll not go back?"

"I'm a dead man if I do. Josh will tell him a whole load of crap. Josh and me, we ain't what you'd call friends."

"Let me get this straight. You're willing to accompany us both to Riverneck?"

"I am."

"And then what?"

"I haven't rightly thought that far ahead, ma'am. I don't know. Find a job. I'm a carpenter by trade."

Eyes half-closing, she regarded him so keenly he grew uncomfortable, shifting his own gaze to settle on the boy with the gun, a sight he found only marginally less disconcerting.

"If you try anything, I'll kill you."

He forced a smile. "Ma'am, I've done with all of that. Trust me."

"I'm not the trusting kind, mister. Not anymore." She slurped down several mouthfuls of stew before adding, "My name's Violet, by the way."

And he sat as she finished off her stew and considered if his decision to help her might prove the most dangerous of his life.

Seventeen

The snow came down in a thick wall as Josh rode into the town of Glory, bent double with cold, hands stuffed inside his coat, the horse walking its own chosen direction. At the livery stable, he got down, every movement a struggle, and the young boy took the horse inside without a word.

Stepping into the Golden Nugget saloon, he crossed immediately to the fire, unaware of anyone else, not caring for anything but the desire to be warm. His coat was stiff with cold, his fingers blue, eyes watery, everything around him out of focus. The fire drew him to its flames and he knelt down in front of it, moaning and rocking himself backwards and forwards, luxuriating in the warmth.

"Where's Clifton?"

The voice came to him from a distance, a strange, hollow sound, not at all human.

"I *said*, where's Clifton?" And, this time, a heavy boot in the ribs followed the sharply delivered words.

Josh span around, looking up into the face of Shelby, who sneered down at him, malevolent, cruel eyes narrowed into mere slits. He swayed slightly, lips thick and wet. Drunk.

"He went after the woman."

"Woman?" Placing his hands on his hips, Shelby leaned backwards, sucking in a huge breath, "So where's the money?"

"We – I mean, *she*, the woman, I mean – Hell, there was no money! Shelby, we tried to—"

"What in the hell do you mean, *no money*?" With his voice cracking, Shelby shot out both hands, gripped Josh by the lapels of his coat and hauled him to his feet. Jutting his face close, Shelby hissed through clenched teeth, "You better tell me what the hell you mean, Josh, and you better tell me quick."

Averting his eyes, trying to hold his breath as the stench of whisky from the depths of Shelby's mouth wafted over him, Josh struggled to batten down the surging dread building up from within. "She'd gone. Run off, with her boy. Clifton, he took to following her, to bring her back."

"Following her? You mean, he's gone after her, across country?"

"Yes. That's what I mean. Sweet Jesus, Shelby, we had no choice. We spoke to the old woman and she was as crazy as a bat in a barn, but she told us, told us Forbes had no money, least not what she knew of, and that the woman, she'd got up and left."

"Where?" He shook Josh violently. "*Where* did she go?"

"Oh shit, Shelby, I don't know! That's why Clifton went after her, to find her and bring her back."

"Across the open plain? Are you stupid? It's alive with Redskins! Holy God Almighty, I knew I should have gone myself." And with that, he pushed Josh away and swung around. He went to the bar and helped himself to a drink from the whisky bottle lying open on the counter. As the fiery liquid hit his throat, he gasped, head down, allowing it to percolate through his insides. He then took another mouthful. "You're a fucking idiot, Josh. Both of you are. How long ago did you leave him?"

"A day. It's not so very far, Shelby. I didn't hesitate none, but came straight back. Clifton will be fine. He can look after himself."

"He's an idiot," muttered Shelby as he took another drink and turned. "I should kill you, you moron. But I won't. I need you. The town committee got together and decided to send a telegram to Laramie, asking them to send a U.S. Marshal."

"Oh shit."

"Exactly. In this blizzard, I doubt they'll be coming all that soon, so we have time to make ourselves ready. I cannot say I am not disappointed in you, Josh, 'cause I am. I need that money, goddamnit, and I am not prepared to let this go unpunished. You let me down, the both of you."

"Shelby, for the love of God, I told you – there is no money."

"How do I know that's true, you piece of lying shit?"

Josh, his throat dry, struggled to keep himself from keeling over. He swayed from side to side, pressing a hand to his forehead, the room spinning. "Shit, I don't feel so good."

"Best get him wrapped up in bed," came a voice and through a haze of distorted images and strange, otherworldly sounds, Josh saw an angel descending the stairs, her long legs and tightly drawn waist bringing an urgent burning to his loins.

"Get the hell back upstairs, Stella," said Shelby, voice a little slurred now, not helped by another swig of whisky. "I'll come and attend to you shortly."

"Shelby, you couldn't attend to your own pissing right this moment." She took the banister rail at the foot of the stairs and used it to twist herself onto the floor, her smile wide and inviting. "My, you look cold, Josh. And you're all feverish." She went over to him and, to Josh, she seemed to float on a golden cloud, her body backlit by an intense beam of pure white. Closing his eyes, he breathed in her sweet perfume, the fire in his loins growing stronger with every passing second.

"You're close to passin' out, darlin'. Let me take you to bed."

Her arms slipped around his waist and he swooned into her soft, yielding body.

"Stella, you get your goddamned hands off of him!"

"Oh shut up, Shelby. Can't you see he's ill? He's caught a chill and needs rest. You stay down here with your bottle, I'll see to him."

"You'll do no such thing," he blurted, knocking away the whisky bottle with a violent swipe, projecting it all the way down the bar to tip over the far end to fall and smash on the floor. He lurched forward, groping for the Smith and Wesson in his waistband. "I'll kill you both, damn your eyes."

"Shelby," said Stella, lifting out Josh's own revolver and pointing it unerringly towards the other, "just shut up and let me tend to him."

Gaping, Shelby tried again to find his gun, but his hands missed the mark and he fell down on his backside and sat there, a thin line of spittle drooling from his lips. "Shit, I'm drunk."

"You're always drunk," she hissed, and pressed Josh closer to her bosom, "Come on, you, let's get you into bed."

"Yes please," Josh managed, wrapped up in a cocoon of warmth, French perfume and delicious sensuality.

Stella giggled and slowly crossed to the staircase, keeping Josh close, but his revolver even closer.

Eighteen

At Riverneck, with the sun dropping down below the horizon and the wind building, they checked into a moth-eaten, crumbling hotel, the little old man behind the reception desk scrawling their names in a huge ledger, spidery script crawling across the page. "Don't get many visitors nowadays," he said, voice tremulous, "not since the mine gave out. No one bothers to come here no more. You folks aim to stay long?"

Clifton shrugged, twisting his neck to look across to the woman and child standing there, silent, resentful. "One night. Tomorrow we'll be moving on."

"We're aiming to go to Patsy and Wilbur Wright's homestead."

"Ah," the old man dropped his eyes to the ledger, studying the names Clifton had scrawled again. "Patsy and Wilbur. Good, good. Well, if you'll be wanting anything to eat, I can offer only cold meats. Breakfast is at seven-thirty." With his pencil between finger and thumb he pointed across the narrow foyer to a handsome looking grandfather clock standing against the wall. "Time is struck on the hour and every half hour after that, so listen out for the chimes or you'll miss the eating time." He took out a key from the set of wooden boxes behind him and dropped it on the desk. "Second floor, number four."

"Is there anyone else here?"

"Nobody stayed here for nigh on two years. I told you, business is bad. There is rumour of a stage passing through here, but you know what rumours are like. But I'm hopeful."

Clifton scooped up the key and made to go up the stairs. He stopped when neither Violet nor Leo seemed ready to move. "You coming?"

"You say there's no one else?" Violet asked the old man.

"Like I said …"

"Then you'll have another room. For myself and the boy."

The old man shifted his gaze across to Clifton, grunted, then fished out another key. "It'll cost you extra."

She stepped over and snatched the key from his gnarled fist. "Now why am I not surprised by that?"

* * *

In the morning, having missed breakfast, they met on the steps to the hotel and all three stared out into the street. "You pay him?" she asked.

"I did."

"My folks, they live not far. I appreciate what you've done for me and the boy, helping us across and all. If I appear ungrateful, it is simply due to my lack of trust in menfolk. It's nothing personal against you."

"I understand. Having lived through what you have with that Forbes character, your reactions are wholly justified. Might I ask, however, if I could accompany you? I'm sure the threat of danger is past, but I would wish to speak to your kin, perhaps discover if there may be any chances for employment hereabouts."

"From the look of it, I doubt it, but you could try. Maybe if that stage is a reality, they'll need some help."

So they made their way slowly out of town, Clifton astride his horse and Violet with her son on their large, robust mule, aware of eyes searching them from behind windows. Riverneck was little more than a single street, the buildings evenly spaced, large gaps between each one, and the wind howled across the crudely fitted wooden walls and along the warped boardwalks. Ill-fitting doors clattered and groaned and near the end, in the bat-winged doorway of a saloon, a tall man leaned on his elbows and studied them, whistling tunelessly to himself.

Clifton caught his stare and a buzz ran down his spine into his bowels; he quickly looked away.

The doors creaked open and the man stepped out. Despite the cold, he wore a pressed white shirt, with bootlace tie, black waistcoat and matching trousers. Bear-headed, he took a moment to light a cigar and puffed at it noisily before tossing away the spent match. "Morning," he said, cheerful enough.

Clifton doffed his hat whilst Violet remained unperturbed, eyes fixed ahead. Leo, of all of them, studied the man with keen interest. "Look at those guns," he whispered.

And Clifton did. A pair of ivory handled Colts, high up on the man's hip, butts turned inwards. He quickly looked away again, kicking his horse's flank lightly to speed the animal up. "Let's move on," he said between his teeth and Violet, without any reaction, did the same. Before long the town of Riverneck was far behind them.

From a distance, all seemed perfectly normal. Even the dog, lying on the porch, the breeze causing the swing to gently sway, with the wind chimes taking up a becalming, musical accompaniment. Clifton could almost taste the sponge cakes, the apple turnover, could almost smell the sweet aroma of cedar wood crackling in the grate. Gleaming white walls, black tiled roof of slate. This was high living and Clifton couldn't help but smile.

Without any warning, Violet pulled her mule up short and snapped her head towards Clifton. A ghastly pallor overtook her flesh, eyes protruding, mouth quivering. "Something's not right."

Tensing, Clifton's hand instinctively dropped to his holster. He cursed on finding it empty. Violet said something to Leo, who reached inside his woollen padded jacket and produced the Remington. Without a word, Clifton took it and checked the load. His eyes met hers. "Are you sure?"

"I can feel it."

In silence, he eased himself from the saddle and approached the house, alert, ready to bring the gun to bear if need be.

Ten more paces and he realised the dog was dead. He stopped, holding up his hand in case Violet decided to join him. Scanning the lower storey windows, his eyes roamed across the roof and the further two windows jutting out from it. He thought he saw the flickering of a net curtain, but he could not swear to it. Taking a breath, he eased back the hammer of his revolver and took the first step leading to the porch.

Each step creaked ominously, sounding loud in that frosted land, but no other sound came to him. Stepping to the side of the door, he flattened himself against the adjacent wall and looked across at her. She'd brought out the single barrelled shotgun and sat, shrouded in her black clothes, stark against the barren, open fields behind her.

Reaching across he gripped the door handle and turned it. He heard the catch moving clear and pushed the door open, immediately springing back to cover against the wall.

There was no response, no gunshot, scream or voice demanding who he was, how he dared enter unannounced. Swallowing hard, he shot a glance towards the dog, its head on its outstretched paws, eyes open, the blood pooling around the body; frozen blood, old.

He slid down the wall and waited, on his haunches, counting off the seconds. At the count of three, he rolled into the gloom of the interior.

* * *

Violet sat, breathing through her mouth, straining to hear. She saw Clifton disappearing inside and expected some sort of follow-up, but there was none. Leo pressed himself against her, his voice tiny and afraid, "I don't like this, mama. Can't we go back to the hotel?"

"Hush now, darlin'. It'll be all right."

"But you don't know that."

"No. But I'm sure—"

She stopped abruptly and twisted at an approaching sound to see a rider moving slowly towards them. All in black, his hat tall crowned, it took her some time to recognise him. By the time her doubts disappeared, with his features so evident, a new fear boiled up from within. "Leo. Go and take the mule over to the side of the house."

"Take the mule? What do you mean?"

She looked down at his enormous, doe eyes and forced a smile. "Please, darlin', just lead the mule over to the corner and keep out of sight." With that, she jumped down, her bent knees cushioning the shock of the landing, the ground iron hard, earth frozen solid beneath the top soil.

"Isn't he the man from town?" asked Leo, even his innocent voice growing sharp, tense. "The one who was watching us?" She nodded. Without any further argument Leo sprang down, keeping hold of the reins and, with a forceful tug, pulled the mule away, leaving his mother to stand rooted, the shotgun across her body. He never once stopped staring at the man in black's approach.

"That's far enough, mister," she said through gritted teeth, swinging the shotgun around to cover the rider, now less than ten paces away.

He pulled back on the reins and stopped, both hands resting on the pommel, head tilted. "Awful jumpy, aren't we?"

"What the hell are you doing following us?"

He took a moment, considering her words, chewing his bottom lip. "Well, that's an interesting theory. Following you? Why would I be following you?"

"You saw us back in town, didn't you? We seemed to take your interest."

"Strangers are few and far between in Riverneck. I was only trying to be friendly."

"And you coming out here? What's your explanation for that?"

He regarded her with a cold stare. "Ma'am, I don't believe there are any laws which say I can't take a ride in the country if I so wish."

"In this weather, in this cold?" She eased back the hammer. "You know who owns this place?"

"That I don't," he said before adjusting himself in the saddle, the creaking of leather filling the air. "Ma'am, I'd ask you to be real careful with that old gun of yours."

"Tell me who you are, first, and what you want."

"Well," he took a deep breath, "it's like this … My name is—"

But his personal introduction was cut short as a body erupted through one of the top storey windows in a great explosion of shattered glass, landing with a sickening thud on the hard-packed, unforgiving ground. Violet gasped and Leo, running from around the corner of the house, screamed in horror. The body lay on its back, legs twitching, eyes rolling into the back of the head.

It was Clifton.

Nineteen

Simms noticed Martinson and his horse struggling through the blizzard long before he heard his voice calling across the snow-covered prairie, "Hello in there, get the damned coffee on before I'm frozen solid!"

Closing the door behind him, the detective waited on the porch, smothered in his thick overcoat, gripping the collar tight around his throat.

"It must be desperate news for you to come out in this," said Simms once his friend had safely stabled his horse in the barn at the rear.

Stamping his feet on the porch, Martinson shook the snow from his shoulders and thrust a piece of paper into Simms's outstretched hand. "Telegram. It said urgent, so I thought …"

Simms stepped aside to allow his merchant friend to enter the warmth of the cabin. Coming up behind him, Simms called across to Annabelle, "You can make coffee?"

"If you untie these bonds, I can do anything."

Grunting, Simms moved over and tugged at the leather cords around the woman's ankles. When freed, she rubbed hard at the slightly chafed skin and wandered over to the stove in the far corner. Martinson watched before turning a quizzical eye towards the Pinkerton. Simms shrugged, "Don't ask."

Whilst Martinson pulled off his coat and sat down with a deep sigh in the easy chair beside the fire, Simms read the note. It didn't take long. He folded up the paper neatly and considered it for a moment. "They want me to go across to Glory."

"Who? Your office?"

"Seems like the town council have made another request to Laramie for a U.S. Marshal."

"Another one?"

"They requested one a little while back, when Jeremiah Malpas, the judge, was found dead. I guess, as I'm closer, I'll be the equivalent."

Martinson, with his palms stretched out towards the fire, gave a non-committal nod. "I doubt you'll be going very far in this blizzard."

"You did."

"Yes, but Glory's a lot farther than Bovey is. It's a good day's ride, even when the trail is clear."

"Well, I have to take the woman into town, so now is as good a time as any."

Over by the stove, Annabelle busied herself with preparing the coffee and didn't appear to be listening. Martinson, watching her keenly, asked, without turning his head from her, "So, what did she do?"

"Maybe another time – when we're alone."

With his eyes widening, Martin looked at his old friend, "Very mysterious."

"No, not at all. Horrifying is how I'd put it."

The sound of coffee pouring into tin cups cut through the icy silence. Moving across the room, Simms took up the two cups and handed one to Martinson. They both drank in silence.

For the rest of the morning, Simms kept Annabelle close by him as they saddled up their horses and packed up some supplies. Martinson, luxuriating in front of the fire, was content enough to do nothing. When Simms did return, his face ruddy with the cold, his coat steaming in the heat of the room, Martinson stood up and pulled a face. "You seem anxious enough to get going."

"The telegram. I didn't tell you the last words."

"Oh? What were they?"

In answer, Simms passed it across to his friend. "I take it you didn't read it?"

"It was addressed to you."

Simms nodded, the trust between the two men evident. "Read it now."

And Martinson did, his eyes immediately drawn to the final message strip, 'Sheriff murdered'.

Twenty

Most of the room was filled by the enormous man next to the empty fireplace. He wore a crumpled grey shirt, sleeves rolled up over his bulging biceps and, arms crossed, he glared down at Clifton, quivering on the threadbare couch.

In the far corner, huddled together like small, terrified animals, Violet and Leo stared out from wide, frightened eyes. No one spoke until the man in black came in, boots unnaturally loud on the bare wooden floor, his spurs ringing.

"Make up a fire would you, Silas? I'm as cold as a frosted nut on a Christmas morning."

"I don't like Christmas."

"Silas, just make up the damned fire."

The giant grunted and set to his task. Turning, the man frowned towards Violet and her son. "Ma'am, you need to sit down before y'all fall down. And him," he nodded towards Clifton, face like ash, eyes black rimmed, mouth trembling, "I'm not convinced he has much time left before he shrugs off his mortal coil."

"Who the hell are you?"

He arched a single eyebrow. "You don't know?"

"I've never set eyes on you before," said Violet, holding Leo tighter still, "Not since that first time back in town."

"Well, I know you." He chuckled at her bemused expression. "We been watching you, Silas and me. Been watching you coming into town and making your way to this here shit heap of a house. Been watching you unload your mule and stashing away your gold."

Her mouth dropped.

"That's right," he continued. "The first time we saw you, we thought it mighty strange that a woman should be coming into town on her own. Silas here was the one who suggested following you. So we did."

"You're lying!"

"Am I?" He shrugged and moved over to Clifton. He placed a hand on the injured man's forehead. "He's burning up. I reckon he broke both his legs in the fall. Silas, bless him, he don't know his own strength." He stooped down on his haunches, face close to Clifton, whose eyes remained set, unblinking, as if unable to understand what had happened. "Can you hear me, boy? How do you know this lady?"

"He came looking for Daryl."

"Daryl? Who the hell is that?"

"He lived with us. Looked after me and my boy."

"Was he the purveyor of the gold?"

She didn't answer, preferring to look away. Leo twisted in her arms and buried his face into her body.

"Well, this is interesting," said the man and stood up, pulling out one of the revolvers at his hip. "I've a mind to put a bullet in that boy's head if you don't tell me all you know."

Clifton groaned and Silas, in front of the fire, cursed, "Fuck this, Hanson, I can't get the thing to light up."

"You're as useless as a padre in a brothel, you dimwit."

"Don't you go saying such things, Hanson. Goddamnit, if I hadn't—"

"Do shut up, Silas, and put some kindling on those logs. Didn't your papa teaching you nuthin'?"

"He taught me how to plough fields and plant corn, not to do this dumbass shit."

Hanson tutted and motioned towards Violet with his gun. "I'll count to three. If you ain't told me all you know, I'll kill the boy. One …"

"All right," she said, voice bereft of panic or anger; flat, emotionless. "It was his gold. He stored it in the barn of his place. I found it by sheer chance."

"And decided to take it for your own?"

"For me and the boy. I hated that bastard."

"Mm …" Hanson rubbed the barrel of his gun up and down his cheek. "So, what was your plan, to share the loot with lover boy here?"

"He's not my lover. He's just a drifter, looking for Dylan."

"And the gold?"

"And the gold."

Hanson glanced down towards Clifton. "I think he's taken real bad. Maybe those legs of his broke inside and he is bleeding. I saw a man die once because he was bleeding inside. What do you think, Silas?"

With his back to Hanson, continuing to struggle with setting the fire alight, the big man replied with a grunt and a dismissive, "I guess."

"So how did he know about Dylan?"

Stroking the top of Leo's hair, Violet shook her head slightly. "I don't know."

"Now I'm thinking *you* is lying." He aimed the revolver again. "I'm about to reach *two* …"

"I *don't know*," she insisted, pressing the boy ever closer to her. "If I knew I'd tell you. They came, two of them, and they wanted to know where Dylan kept the money. But I wasn't there, I'd already gone and—"

"Lady, *none* of this is making any sense. How could you know they was looking for the money when you wasn't there?"

"He told me. Him," she waggled her figure in the general direction of Clifton, her voice tremulous, close to panic. "He told me they'd shot the old woman too and I didn't know if he was lying or—"

"What old woman?"

"The one who lived in the cabin with us."

Hanson let out a long sigh and slowly holstered his gun. "All right, let's say I believe you – for now."

"I swear to you I'm telling the truth. I have no reason to lie – you have the money, damn your hide."

"Yes, that we do indeed." He smiled and wandered around the back of the couch and peered down at Clifton's body. "You said there was two of them?" She nodded. "So where is the other one?"

"He went back to Glory."

"Glory? So that's where he came from?"

"I know Glory," rumbled Silas, climbing to his feet and stepping back to admire his success at finally lighting the fire. He rubbed his hands together and swung around. "It is a stinking cesspit, no better than Riverneck."

"So these two came out of Glory, looking for the money. But how did they know how to get to you?"

"I guess someone must have told them where Dylan lived."

"And Dylan? Where is he?"

"He's dead."

Hanson raised his eyebrows. "Ah, now it's getting clearer. They killed him, after finding out where his money was, then came looking for it and found his place deserted."

"Then this one came searching for me. I doubt he could find his own pecker in the dark, let alone me. I came upon him and together we rode here, to my brother's place."

"This is your brother's place?"

"It was, before he died."

"I see. So, you chose an empty house to stow away your ill-gotten gains?"

"Not mine – Dylan's."

"And where he get it all?"

"Banks and the like. He was with a gang. He didn't tell me much, but I got that from him."

"And this gang – I'm guessing they are the ones who came out of Glory, looking for their share." He folded his arms. "So maybe they'll come out here, looking for the rest?"

"Maybe, but I doubt it – they don't know anything about this place. How could they?"

"I don't think I can take that risk. Seems like our best plan, dear Silas, is to take the fight to the enemy. I don't want to be bushwhacked on the trail."

"Makes sense to me," said the big man. "What do we do with her?"

Hanson chuckled and moved his hand to one of his guns.

Violet threw out her hands. "Listen, Mister, I just want what is rightfully mine. Give me enough money for me and the boy to set ourselves up and we can all walk away from this."

"We could all walk away from it right now," smiled Hanson. "I have no desire to share any of our money, with you or anyone else."

"There's more of it," she blurted. "I could show you. *If …*" She let her words hang in the air, enticingly.

Hanson exchanged a quick look with Silas. "A lot more?"

"More than is here, that's for sure."

"Well, little lady, you tell me where it is and we—"

"No. No, I'll go and get it and bring it back."

"Do you take me for a dimwit? As soon as you're out of sight, you will be flying from here like a rooster chased by a fox!"

"I wouldn't get far."

"Maybe, maybe not. So, here's what we'll do – you can go, but you leave the boy behind."

Instinctively, Leo clung closer to her. She ruffled his hair and shook her head. "I won't do that."

He shrugged and drew his gun. "Then you'll all die."

"And you won't get another penny."

Hanson paused, cocked his head and contemplated the woman for a long time.

"I'll go with her," said Silas, breaking the impasse. "I'll make sure she comes back."

Hanson nodded, continuing to pull out his gun, which he aimed with great care at Clifton's head. "If you don't come back, he dies."

"I'll come back," she said. "I don't want him to die."

"Is that a fact?"

"Yes. It is."

He held her gaze, grunted and slipped his gun back in its holster again. "If you get the sense anything is wrong, Silas, you kill them. Both of them."

Silas shrugged and moved towards the door, "And to think I only just got that fire going."

And with Hanson's laughter ringing around the room, Silas took Violet by the shoulder and led her and the boy out into the cold daylight.

Twenty one

In the town of Glory, Shelby, having ordered Josh to call what remained of the town council to a meeting, stood in front of his bedroom window, gazing down to the street. The clasp rattled as the wind came rolling between the wooden slatted buildings, snowdrifts gathering beneath the boardwalks. Despite the cold he remained bare-chested, quietly smoking a thin cheroot, deep in thought.

Behind him, still in the bed, Stella moaned, yawned and stretched. She took a few moments, smacking her lips, yawning again before she mumbled, "What time is it?"

"Almost noon," replied Shelby, looking at her over his shoulder. He chuckled. "You've missed the best part of the day. The morning."

"I know a lot about mornings," she said and swung her legs from out of the covers and sat on the edge of the bed. Yawning, she ran her fingers through her tangled hair. "Early ones."

She stood up and padded across the room to him, her naked body alabaster white. He ran his arm around her slim waist, skin as smooth as porcelain. Leaning into him, she kissed his neck whilst he returned to considering the street.

"What are you waiting for?"

"I want to talk to them, so I'm waiting for them to show."

"Who?"

"What's left of the council."

"I don't understand ..."

He grinned. "You've no need to. You'll know soon enough."

"I thought I heard voices in the night. Someone was shouting."

"Yes, that was me and that weasel Jones, the bank manager. He came here, pounding on the door, demanding to speak with me." He grinned. "Well he did, and then some."

Again, her frown creased her lovely face. "You're making too many enemies, from what I can tell."

"Well, let's just say we had a disagreement. He threatened me. Nobody does that."

"So, what happened?"

He spat a single, dismissive laugh. "What always happens when people cross me."

Her body stiffened and she slipped away from him, reaching for her gown and drifting over to the washing basin standing on the dresser. Shelby, never taking his eyes off her, wondered how she might react when she went downstairs to the bar room. All things considered, and he considered much, he thought it best if she remained in the bedroom until the meeting was over.

He returned to looking outside. A slight movement at the far end of the main street caught his attention and he squinted through the gathering blizzard, trying to make out what the approaching shapes were. As he strained, Stella called out, "I need a drink." He whirled, went to shout out for her to stop, but she was gone and, shoulders sagging, he leaned back against the cold windowpane, let out a long sigh and waited.

He didn't have to wait long.

A single ear-piercing scream broke the stillness of the building, causing the window behind him to shake more than the wind had done. In a flurry, he swept up his gun belt and jacket and burst out of the room at a run.

The naked body of the bank manager dangled upside down, attached by chains running through two hooks from the ceiling. Shelby, having cut the man's throat, positioned a metal pail under the corpse, allowing the blood to drip and collect inside. Jones gently swayed, his putrid white flesh having taken on the appearance of a huge, loathsome, puckered maggot, blue-veined with a blue tongue poking out from between swollen, purple lips. Unrecognisable as someone anyone would know, Shelby had thoughtfully tied a wooden notice around Jones's neck, his name scrawled across the plaque in red paint. Now, coming down the stairs, he paused to admire his handiwork before Stella's second, fearful shriek wrested his attention. Slumped on her knees, face in hands, body trembling in horror. Every time she'd peep out between her fingers, another scream would follow. Shelby, finding the noise too much, strode over to her and cracked his revolver across her temple, dumping her to the floor where she lay, whimpering.

As he went to cross to the bar, the doors burst open and Josh came in, with what remained of the town council close behind, all steaming breath and bunched up shoulders. As their stares centred on the charnel house before them, a shocked, stony silence settled over them. Shelby ignored them, filling up a glass with his first whisky of the day. He threw it down in one, turned and surveyed the collection of shocked faces. He sniggered, "My oh my, how horrified you all look. Not the thing for a Sunday morning is it?"

Perhaps not surprisingly, Mrs Hubert was the first to recover, but not in a way Shelby would ever have thought. She flew at him, taking him totally unawares, both set of nails raking down his face as her legs wrapped around him like a vice, sending him crashing to the floor. Straddling him, she rained down blow after blow into his head, screaming, "Murdering bastard, filthy murdering bastard!"

A collective gasp sprang out from the others. Josh, reacting first, took a step forward to help his friend, his gun coming out of its holster. At that moment, Howard, the town mayor, no doubt emboldened by Mrs Hubert's attack, grappled Josh around the waist, twisting him to the ground. Frantic, overtaken by a wild, ill-thought desire for vengeance, Howard's fists pummelled into Josh's side. But Josh was no stranger to violence. Younger and far stronger than the mayor, he easily broke free, landing a punch of his own across the man's jaw, which quickly took all the fight out of him. Climbing to his feet, Josh slammed two or three kicks into the man's body and stepped back, breathing hard.

Mrs Hubert stood up. No longer the prim, polite pillar of Glory's somewhat tarnished society, her dress ripped, blood leaking from broken knuckles, hair falling lank and unruly over her face, she turned with controlled slowness towards Josh. In her fist was Shelby's gun.

"Now hold on," said Josh, palms outstretched. He took a quick glance towards his own gun, lying next to the groaning Howard. "Lady, you don't want to—"

She shot him through the chest, blowing his body backwards. However, the recoil itself was so powerful, so unexpected, it threw her backwards too, her spine jarring against the corner of the bar with a sickening crunch. Yelping, she stumbled sideways, the gun dropping from her fingers, both hands pressing into her back, a movement that allowed Shelby the opportunity to sweep up his revolver and bring it to bear.

"No, Shelby!"

Blinking, he looked up to see Stella, feet planted wide apart. From somewhere she'd found a rifle, a short-barrelled carbine to be precise. It was primed and cocked and it was pointing directly at him. He groaned and collapsed unconscious to the ground.

Twenty two

By late morning, the snow, which up until then had been little more than the occasional flurry, came down far more thickly, reducing visibility to around twenty paces. Astride her mule, Violet twisted to peer towards Silas, whose own mount appeared to buckle under the weight of its burden. Silas truly was an enormous individual. She did not believe she had ever come across a man so large. Despite his size and his frightening strength, he appeared to be suffering dreadfully from the cold. Huddled in his coat, he shivered constantly, his great bulk quivering like the precursor to an earthquake. His skin had taken on a deathly pallor, blue-grey like the surrounding rocks. She doubted he would last much longer and decided to take a circuitous route to her old cabin, one which would greatly delay their arrival.

But the snow proved the enemy to both. With the well-worn trail disguised beneath a heavy, white blanket, they soon became hopelessly lost and Silas, mustering whatever strength remained, ordered her to stop and find cover amongst a cluster of nearby trees.

They kept the horses close, dismounting and leading them through the trees. Here, with the snow unable to penetrate quite so thickly and the temperature a little higher, Silas seemed to recover somewhat. He found a clearing and managed to start a fire, using a flint and steel he fished out from one of his saddlebags. Watching, slumped up against a tree trunk, Violet held Leo close to her, drawing her coat around him, luxuriating in the warmth his small body afforded. "You're a skilled man," she said, impressed.

Silas grunted, stooping close to blow at the kindling he'd gathered, giving it the chance to catch alight. He fed the tiny flames more pieces of twigs and coarse grass, taking his time, careful not to extinguish the fragile fire. "Learned it all in the army," he said. "Learned lots of things in the army."

He had his back to her and she could see how his muscles strained against the material of his coat. Her eyes settled on one of many fallen branches close by. As the fire crackled and he fed it several thicker logs, she gently eased Leo to one side and moved forward.

He turned. Perhaps some sixth sense, or the soft pad of her feet, forewarned him, but he brought up his arm instinctively as the first blow came down, all of her strength behind the swing. She knew he would take a lot of killing, being so large, so she held nothing back. The branch smashed down across his forearm, shattering bone. He squealed and fell back over the fire. Perhaps due to his coat being so damp from the snow, his clothes did not catch alight, but nevertheless, he rolled over, panic stricken, a move which allowed her a perfect target. She cracked the branch across his head. Stunned, he went down, breath exploding from his mouth in a loud groan. She hit him again and again, not stopping until his brains drooled out from his shattered skull and his great body lay still.

It took all of her remaining strength to drag his great bulk away from the fire. She then took to rekindling it, desperate for the feeble flames to take hold. Concentrating so hard on her endeavours, she put everything else out of her mind except the desire to survive. With little hope of picking up the trail in such deep snow, she knew if the fire did not take, they would freeze to death out here in the wilderness. So she struggled with everything she had whilst Leo sat against the tree, quietly sobbing, wide-eyed and shivering. She forced a smile towards him, but he did not return it and she realised in that single, dreadful moment, nothing but their doom awaited them.

Twenty three

Martinson stoked up the wood-burner whilst Simms handed over two blankets to the woman, stepped outside the small cell and locked it. Miller, the Sheriff, stood chewing his bottom lip, hands on hips, a dark look on his face. "I'm not happy about any of this," he said.

"Nor me," said Simms, hanging the keys of a nearby hook. "I'd much rather have her in my office, but as I don't have a cell—"

"That's not what I mean and you know it."

"I know she's guilty of some pretty awful things, Miller, and when the Judge arrives, I'll put forward my case."

"I'm talking about jurisdiction, Simms. This is my town. I can't allow you to go high-tailing around the Territory like some vigilante, doling out your own kind of justice. We have laws here, goddamnit."

"You know the arrangements, Miller. They've all been agreed with the government."

"The Government has no jurisdiction out here either."

"So only you have, is that what you mean?"

"Damned right." He puffed out his chest. "I'm the town's elected law officer. I want it recorded I am not in agreement with you treating this woman the way you have without due process. You're a witness to this, Swede."

"So recorded," said Martinson from across the far side of the room, rubbing his hands together in front of the stove.

"I need to go across to Glory," said Simms. "Seems they are having some trouble and it's doubtful the Marshal will be able to get there until the weather eases off. I'm asking you to keep this woman here, Miller, under lock and key until I return."

"I'll give you three days, Simms. I can't allow her to remain here without charges being brought, and you seem reluctant to tell me anything."

"I'll never get back here in three days and you know it – not in these conditions."

"Well, that's all I'm giving you."

"Joe," said Martinson, stepping up close, "I think maybe you're taking your duty a tad too far. We all know the Detective's reputation. If he says he has just cause, then he has just cause."

"Has he told you what she is supposed to have done?"

Martinson screwed up his mouth, "Not exactly, but that's not the point."

"Well, it is to me." His eyes narrowed. "Four days."

"I'll leave at first light," said Simms, "so let us make it five. Please."

"I'll prepare her meals," put in Martinson quickly. "Damn it, I'll even sit in here with her if it makes you feel better."

"It doesn't," snapped Miller, "but, very well … Five days as from tomorrow. On the morning of the sixth, I'm letting her go." He shot a vicious glance towards Martinson. "You'll stay here, day and night, and make sure she is kept warm and well fed. She is your responsibility and, if anything happens to her, you'll answer for it."

"Nothing will happen," said Martinson and nodded across to Simms. "When you get back, you'll need to move quick in order to get this woman convicted."

Simms took a breath but surrendered to the inevitable. "All right. I'll get a telegram off to the circuit judge at Fort Bridger, then prepare some supplies for the journey. Ordinarily it would take me less than a day to ride across to Glory, but the way the snow is moving in, I doubt I'll make it in two." He took up his coat and buttoned it up to the collar, gave a nod to Martinson and went out.

His own office was little more than a few strides down the main street and, when he got there, he took a moment to admire the repairs made to his door. Inside, the office was bitter cold. Not much had changed since the last time he was there and the empty whisky bottle standing on his desk proved a grim reminder of how deep into the mire of despair he'd fallen. Swallowing down thoughts of Noreen and their child, he pulled down his carbine from the rack, found a piece of paper in the top drawer of his desk and scratched out a brief request for the circuit judge to come to Bovey at his earliest convenience. Miller would not hesitate to let the woman go, so Simms had no recourse but to take her back to his own ranch house on his return. Five days. He leaned on his desk and peered at his carbine. Five days. He'd need every ounce of luck if he was to make it. Whatever was happening over at Glory couldn't be so bad to warrant him staying there for more than a day, so perhaps there was a chance. He did not relish tracking Annabelle down again, but track her he would if Miller released her. Towards that end, he made the decision to first visit Deep Water and recruit him.

Twenty four

Snapping his bag shut, Doctor Hennesey studied Josh for a moment before getting to his feet and looking across the room to Stella, standing against the wall, chewing her nails, tear stains running down her cheeks. "Will he be all right?"

"That, I cannot tell," he said. "The piece of lead is still in there, but I daren't attempt to extract it, not yet. But he's strong and I suspect he will rally in the next day or two. Then I'll take a second look." He waddled across the room, a short man of tremendous girth. At the door he paused, solemn faced. "Stella, I don't wish to pry …"

She looked at him, eyes wet, nose red from holding a handkerchief there too long. "What?"

"The man downstairs, I think he may need attention also."

"He's drunk. He's always drunk."

"He's also fairly badly beaten."

"Yes, well …" She sniffed loudly, walked past him to the bed and knelt down. She stroked Josh's head. She did not look up when the door opened and closed, but waited until the sound of the doctor's footsteps receded. Only then did she lean forward and plant a kiss on the wounded man's head. He moaned softly and she smiled, stood up and went out into the corridor.

At the foot of the stairs, Shelby sat slumped in a chair, eyes closed, whisky glass held loosely in one hand. Over by the door, Mrs Hubert said farewell to the doctor. When she turned, her eyes alighted on Stella.

"Have you still got his gun?"

Mrs Hubert gave a single nod. Reaching the bottom step, Stella shot a quick glance at Shelby before moving around the bar counter and selecting a brandy bottle from the shelf. She filled a glass and took a large mouthful. "What do you think we should do now?"

"We wait for the Marshal. And for justice." She leaned across the top of the double-swing doors, her breath steaming in the cold air. "My only fear is he won't be able to get across the prairie in this ghastly weather."

"Why not kill him now?"

Mrs Hubert turned, frowning. "We're not animals."

"No, but I saw the way you attacked him. I reckon you would have killed him if you had the chance. You tried to do it to Josh. What's the difference?"

With her face colouring, she snapped her head away again. "I didn't know what I was doing. I'm sorry for what I did."

"Are you?"

"Yes. I am. Do you think Josh will recover?"

"Doctor says maybe. Two days and he'll be back, then he'll know more."

"In two days we could all be dead anyway. If he recovers ..." She looked again at Shelby, face ugly in a scowl of anger. "If he ever sobers up, I think the first thing he'll do is kill me."

"Perhaps that's why we should kill him now. He's unpredictable, like a caged animal. Sooner or later he'll feel the urge to escape, then he'll be even more dangerous."

"I thought you had feelings for him?"

Stella cackled, tipped the bottle and refilled her glass. "Lady, I'm a whore. I don't do relationships. So long as he pays, he gets whatever he needs and that's as far as it goes."

"And the other one, the one I shot?"

Shrugging, Stella swirled the brandy around the glass, studying it intensely. "Maybe there could have been a chance for me and him, but ..." She let the words hang in the air then quickly threw the drink down her throat. "Shelby talked about money. Lots of money, that the sheriff stole from him. You know anything about that?"

"He mentioned something similar to us before he started killing everyone."

"Josh said he and the other one, Clifton, they went out looking for it, but couldn't find it. I think that's what changed everything for Shelby. I reckon we could find the money, if we put our minds to it."

"Such a course would make us as bad as they are."

"But it would sure make us a damn sight richer."

From outside, a distant rumbling grew noticeably louder and Stella came around the counter to join Mrs Hubert at the door.

From down the far end of the street marched a group of townsfolk, moving as one, a large, rolling black cloud against the stark white of the snow covered ground. At their head strode Norton Springer, accompanied by a large man clutching a dangerous looking club.

"That doesn't look good," said Stella.

"No," said Mrs Hubert, nodding towards Shelby, sitting bent double, a thin trail of spittle drooling from his mouth, "certainly not for him."

Twenty five

In the end, Hanson grew bored stomping around the empty house, put his revolver against Clifton's head, shielded his face from the inevitable spray of blood and blew the suffering man's brains out. Hanson saw it as an act of kindness, so didn't trouble himself by lingering on the event for too long. Gathering together the bags of money he'd found, he went outside, struggling through the snow, and tied them to the back of the mule sheltering in the lean-to stable. Glancing towards the sky, he pondered on his decision to leave, weighing up the alternatives. He knew there were none. There was no food remaining in the house, with very little wood to keep the fire burning. Within a few days he would die, frozen solid next to Clifton's corpse. Damn this world and everything in it, he cursed, hauling himself up into the saddle and leading horse and mule out into the freezing weather.

He made good going, the trail not as snowbound as he feared. Above him, patches of blue sky broke through the almost universal white, which lightened his heart. When the snow ceased to fall, he felt positively joyful and grinned inanely at the prospect of reaching Silas and the girl and increasing his treasure trove. Estimating the value of the gold and silver stuffed into the heavy bags slapping reassuringly against the mule's rump, he reached a figure in excess of twenty thousand dollars. Enough money for a man to live comfortable for the rest of his life. However, being a naturally greedy man, Hanson would never be satisfied until he had it all. So with shoulders hunched and stare set on the trail snaking before him, he continued resolutely forward.

Soon the trail wended its way amongst black trunked trees, skeletal branches intertwining with each other to form a sort of shelter against the worst of the weather. Nothing moved amongst the undergrowth; animals, knowing the sense of not emerging into the cold, were buried deep underground, snuggled up warm and safe. Not for the first time on his solitary journey, Hanson wished he too sheltered somewhere warm. Thoughts of roaring fires and hot coffee laced with whisky brought him little comfort. The reality of his situation forced its way through his thoughts and the dreadful cold burrowed through his thick overcoat, gripping and twisting his flesh in its agonising embrace.

Sometime in the late afternoon, he noticed a thin stream of smoke spiralling upwards from amongst the trees. Reining in his horse, he sat and considered what to do. Numb with cold, he slid to the ground and, loosely tying the reins around a tree, he drew one of his revolvers and pushed his way deeper into the wood.

The fire no longer burned. All that remained was a feeble smouldering clump of charred logs, oily black smoke wafting upwards. Over to the left, what remained of Silas lay sprawled across the hard earth, now soaked with his blood. His initial instinct was to cross over to his old friend and check for any sign of life, but the sight on his right brought him up sharp, and he snapped back the hammer of his revolver and aimed it towards the woman, sat upright against a tree, her eyes staring directly at him.

She didn't move. Her little boy, half-poking out from her coat, had his hand reaching up to touch his mother's cheek. But he would never do so again, and nor would she respond. When he moved closer and touched her with his foot, Hanson knew straight away. She was frozen solid, the boy along with her, both of them dead.

Swallowing down his panic, Hanson moved through the trees and found their horses. Both were in a deplorable state. He doubted they would survive for much longer, so he rooted through the saddlebags, finding an ample supply of salt-cakes and hard-tack. He fed the ravenous beasts as much as he could, unsaddled them and let them free. With what was left of the meagre supplies, he returned to the bodies, unburdened them of their weapons, powder and shot, then made his way back to his own animals without a second glance.

Three men stood by the two mounts, but not like any other men he had ever seen. Clad in buckskin from head to foot, their faces were painted black, each sported two or three feathers from their long, slick hair. Two of them held long shafted spears in their hands, the third a nocked bow which he held downward facing but slowly brought to bear as Hanson stepped out onto the trail.

The snow slowed him a little, but just enough to give him a chance. He threw himself to his left as the arrow screeched through the still air, shooting the nearest one in the chest with his first bullet. The other two whooped and charged. Hanson, rolling over the snowy blanket beneath him, shot the second three times, fanning the hammer of his Navy in a blur, but the third hit him like a wild cat, knocking the wind out of him.

Terrified by the man's strength, overcome by it, Hanson had no time to fire again. The young brave's hand gripped his gun arm whilst the other reared up, a jagged, evil looking knife in his fist. Hanson squirmed, managed to block the downward strike and got his hands around the attacker's throat. It was a futile effort. With little or no feeling in his fingers, Hanson was unable to put enough force into his grip and the young warrior simply shrugged it off and put his knife deep into Hanson's side. The accompanying burning sensation of sharp metal penetrating flesh drove what strength Hanson had remaining out of him in a rush and he collapsed under the victorious Indian, who stood up, assured and confident.

Hanson lay there, staring towards the sky as the Indian moved around the periphery of his senses, heard him rifling through saddlebags and other belongings. He longed to find the strength to sit up, reach for his gun, but such things were beyond him now. He managed to slip his free hand beneath the folds of his coat and feel around the hot, sticky knife-wound. Luckily, the thickness of his coat's material meant the cut wasn't near as bad as he first believed. Perhaps with a dressing applied the bleeding would soon stop. With this in mind, he pulled away his neckerchief and, bunching it in his fist, did just that, sucking in air through gritted teeth as a new wave of pain washed over his side.

He strained his head to see his revolver lying in the snow, slowly slipping deeper as the heat from the cylinders and muzzle thawed its surroundings. The Indian had kicked it out of reach. A sensible thing to do. Clearly, the brave wanted Hanson to suffer, to lie in the cold, to freeze to death. Rummaging around with bags and bedrolls laid out across the ground, the brave had his back to Hanson but would easily be able to swing around and overcome him again if Hanson tried to reach for the gun. But the solution to this impasse was a simple one, one which the brave probably had not even considered. Moving with deliberate slowness, Hanson brought out his second revolver and shot the brave through the back of the head, then collapsed back into the snow and tried his utmost not to fall asleep.

Twenty six

The journey back from Deep Water's was slow and ponderous, Simms's horse sinking up to its forearms in snow with every step. A resilient and sturdy beast, it kept going and, before long, gained an area comparatively clear and broke into a canter, tossing its head with relief. Deep Water, accepting Simms's request without reservation, set off towards Bovey at the same time, but his way seemed easier and Simms cursed him for that.

Deciding to rest at what remained of Lester Garfield's 'Harness and Saddles' store, Simms turned his horse into the biting wind. Relying on his judgement, gleamed from traversing this area many times, he made the slight detour to what had once been a vibrant trading station. Now, abandoned some years before, what remained was nothing more than a dilapidated, crumbling shell. But at least it had a roof. Simms led his horse inside and tried to make himself as comfortable as possible amongst the various debris, bits of broken furniture and the ghosts of times gone by.

He dreamed in the night.

He stood on a bridge, staring down into the unsullied water, which trickled along at an impossibly slow rate. As he looked, he thought he caught sight of a reflection of Noreen. And as he strained to focus in on her face, she smiled. At once, he turned and saw her, walking away from him, crossing over onto the far bank. Calling out to her, he set off at a run to catch her. But the harder he tried, the more difficult the simple act of running became. It was almost as if he were drowning, a swirling, heavy, glutinous liquid dragging him down. Each step took so much of his strength but, determined, he battled forward, hands reaching out to her swiftly diminishing body. He cried out, "Noreen, wait!" But she didn't turn and when at last he made the far bank, she was out of sight and he fell onto the ground and wept. With his face pressed into his hands, he did not notice the approach of the other person until it was too late and their boot slammed into his side and he cried out again, but in pain this time.

The pain was all too real.

He sat bolt upright, hands instinctively coming up to shield himself from another blow. "Noreen?" he gasped.

"Move real slow, mister."

Simms shook his head and, blinking, peered up to see a young man, encased in a thick bearskin coat, holding an old carbine in his gloved hands. A heavy beard disguised his features, but his lack of years were clearly visible around his smooth eyes. When the girl stepped up next to him, he knew immediately who they were.

"What in the name of God are you—"

"Don't you blaspheme none," shouted the girl. "You just sit real still." She reached inside his coat and groped around until she found the butt of the Colt Dragoon holstered at his hip. She hefted it in her hands. "My, that's a big one." Her eyes widened when she saw the Colt Navy laying beside the saddle Simms had used for a pillow. With a whoop of glee, she picked it up. "Look at me, Curly, I'm a regular gun-toting girl from the wild frontier."

Curly chuckled and, making stabbing moments with the rifle, motioned for Simms to stand up.

"How'd you find me?" asked the detective, dusting off his trousers.

"You told us you were a lawman out of Bovey," said Curly, sneering, well pleased with himself. "So, after we heard all the shooting, we went back into camp, saw all them dead Indians and decided to follow you."

"You buried Pa," said the girl, holding the two guns with some difficulty. She wore over-large fur-lined mitts and decided, after a bout of juggling, to stuff the handguns under her armpit. "That was kind."

Simms shrugged. "So you went to Bovey and discovered I'd left for Glory."

"We need to know where Ma is," said the girl. "We figured she was with you."

"But we was wrong," interjected Curly. "Where is she?"

Without hesitation, Simms told them the truth. "In the jailhouse back at Bovey."

The two young ones exchanged a despairing look. "Ah dang," said Curly, "we'll have to go all the way back."

"She's to stand trial," said Simms, his eyes latched onto Curly. He sensed the young man's discomfort under his furious gaze. "For what she did – for what you *all* did."

"What *we* did?" Curly jerked his head towards Tabatha, "We did nothing wrong, did we honey?"

"Nothing at all. This jackass is trying to trick us with his fancy words and his evil eyes."

"No trick," said Simms, voice even, hands by his side, relaxed, nonchalant. "What you all did was beyond sin. Beyond human decency."

"What in all creation are you talking about?"

Simms studied the young man's bewildered expression and arched a single eyebrow. "Do you seriously expect me to believe you had nothing to do with it?"

"Do with *what*?" blurted the girl; it was then that Simms moved.

His arms streaked out in a blur, catching hold of the rifle barrel, twisting it free from Curly's grip. Taken totally by surprise, the young man had no time to react before Simms rammed the stock straight into his face. He screamed and fell backwards, his nose exploding in a huge splat of bright red blood.

Taken off balance, Tabatha floundered, trying to bring one of the revolvers to bear, but it slipped from between her mittens and she groaned as Simms turned the rifle on her.

He eased back the hammer. "When you have the drop on someone, you'd best take advantage and not hesitate."

With her eyes filling up, she slowly raised her arms. "Mister, I . . ."

Over to the right, rolling around on the floor, Curly's words came gurgling out of his shattered mouth, "Bastard … Bastard …"

"You shut that filthy mouth of yours," the girl snapped and she sniffed loudly, chancing to move her hand and wipe her nose with the back of it. "Mister, we never would have killed you."

"So what was your plan?"

"Well, we – look we thought you had Ma so – well, I guess, we would have gone back with you to Bovey to get her out of that cell."

"I never would have consented to that. She needs to stand trial for what she did." He lowered the rifle but kept the hammer engaged. "You're a God-fearing woman."

Straightening her back, she sniffed again, "I am."

"Then you will give evidence, when the time is right."

"Evidence? What do you mean?"

"At your ma's trial. You must have seen what happened."

"No. No, I swear it, I never. Mister, you have to believe me – if I'd have known, I swear I would have stopped them. But it was Pa. Pa always made the decisions, Ma just went along with it."

"Kind of convenient he's dead, isn't it?"

"I don't lie, Mister. Like you said, I'm God-fearing. I was brought up to always tell the truth, for God, He sees everything and He tallies it all up, so that on the terrible Day of Judgement, we will stand naked and all our—"

"Keep your sermons for your flock, wherever they might be."

"My flock, *our* flock, they're all dead." Her eyes grew ever wider, the tears tumbling down her cheek unchecked. "You know that – you saw them, didn't you."

"I came across the wagons and found the bodies, or what was left of them. When I returned to your parents, I didn't have much chance to question them before we were attacked by a group of Bannock people. "

"So, you saved them? Why would you do that, suspecting what you did?"

"Because I wanted to see them face justice, not have their hair cut from their heads. That's not what I'd call justice. Your parents, they—"

"No," she cried, her voice breaking, body consumed by uncontrolled sobs. She dropped to her knees, hands covering her face. "They're not my parents."

"Then …" Simms shot a glance towards Curly who had managed to drag himself across the room and now sat, knees bunched up, whimpering. "Then who …"

"My parents were back in the other wagons. The ones you found. Lamont, he threatened me that if I spoke about any of it to Lester, Tommy or the others, he'd kill Curly."

"So you did witness it?"

Her hands fell from her face, revealing a bedraggled, broken little girl, all the fight gone from her. "All of it. And if I survive this damned cold, I'll stand up in the courtroom and I'll let the whole world know what they did, the way Annabelle stood by and let it happen."

Simms slumped down into a nearby chair and sat for a long time, staring at the girl and listening to her heartbreaking sobs.

Twenty seven

Arriving at Violet's dilapidated former shack some time after dusk, his entire body gripped in a series of bone-rattling convulsions, Hanson dropped from the saddle. Dismissive of the needs of his horse, he half-crawled up the creaking steps and fell through the door, reeling with the stench that hit him like a fist. Confused, disorientated, he groped like a blind man through the room and crumpled to the floor, shaking with the cold petrifying his bones. He moaned and huddled himself up into a tight ball, teeth chattering, doing his best to find some semblance of warmth in that stinking, filthy room. His hands felt something, a bundle of thick, heavy clothing and he pulled it to him, hoping to get warm again. Too exhausted to care what the heap was, he grunted with the effort but it seemed to work, whatever it was, and a form of contentment moved over him. If he slept, he did not know but when at last he found the strength to open his eyes and sit up, it was light.

He felt better, although the intense cold continued to gnaw away at his bones and when he rubbed his eyes he believed this day would prove to be a good one. Yawning, he stretched out his arms and touched the bulk of clothing next to him.

He turned and saw what the heap actually was and screamed. Rolling away, hands batting away a legion of imaginary demons or flies, he stared towards the putrid remains of an old woman, dark, crusted blood splattered over her frail frame. Quaking, Hanson fell into the far corner and vomited onto the floor. Gasping for breath, he staggered towards the front door, ripped it open and threw himself head first into the deep carpet of snow which spread out in every direction. He stayed there for some time.

Later, when some strength had returned to his limbs, he managed to return indoors. Standing in the doorway, he gazed in disbelief at the corpse, his night-time companion, and fought down the bile rising again to his throat. With a hand pressed against his eyes, he strode through the room and assaulted the various cupboards and shelves, taking up every available wall space in the minuscule kitchen. There was a hand pump and he worked it, hopeful some water would dribble from the spout, but none did. Everything was frozen solid. Ravenous and desperate, he swept his hands across the empty shelves before crumpling to his knees, railing against the gods of fate that had brought him to this terrible juncture in his life. His saddlebags were stuffed with money, he was the richest he had ever been, but what good was wealth with fear, hunger and thirst dominating every wretched moment? So he wept and cursed and tried to free his mind of the inevitable consequences of this foolhardy venture – his own, imminent death.

Thoughts of the money finally forced him to go outside again and find his horse. When he did, nausea again rose up at the scene before him. The poor creature, or what remained of it, lay sprawled out upon the ground, the bulk of its carcass torn apart, entrails spilled out, cracked ribs pointing upwards like frosted, skeletal arms. Rigid, teeth chattering in a face stiff with cold, he scanned the surrounding woods and the pink trails leading into the dark, silent depths. Wolves. There was no other answer. Without another thought, he fought his way through the snow to the dead beast, pulled away the saddlebags and, draping them over his shoulder, turned to head back.

The first howl cut through the eerie silence, turning his stomach to mush. He clawed at the carbine in the sheath next to the saddle, but it refused to budge, the metal fused with the leather. He needed more powder and ball, but what there was in the saddlebags would prove useless. He knew it. So he drew out one of his revolvers as he scanned the surroundings.

His hand shook uncontrollably, the gun heavy in his hand, heavier than he could ever remember. So weak, so helpless. If a pack of wolves emerged from amongst the trees he would not stand a chance, but any sudden movement might just be their signal to attack. So, forcing himself to move as slowly as he was able, he moved back to the shack, keeping his eyes on the tree line, weighed down by the saddlebags, legs plunging deeper into the snow with every step.

Breathing hard, he took the first step up to the entrance. The timbers groaned beneath him and he stopped, waiting, certain something stirred behind him.

Another step and, again, a quiet, controlled rustling. Turning, he squinted across to the tree line. Was that a shadow, or the breeze playing around with the undergrowth? He couldn't tell and, as he went to continue on his approach to the door, the first canine exploded from the woods, snarling and growling, lips drawn back to reveal a vicious set of glistening white teeth, razor-sharp. Hanson stumbled backwards, groping for his revolver and shot the massive wolf in the throat. It yelped once before dropping dead to the ground. Not pausing to give up a prayer of thanks that the weapon worked, he hurled himself through the door and slammed his body back against it as the second animal smashed against the rickety woodwork.

He slid to the floor, listening to the snarls beyond the timber, his pounding heart threatening to explode out of his chest. He strained to listen and heard more wolves joining with their companion, sniffing and pawing at the door. Their heavy snuffling grew as more and more of them arrived, the scent of his fear acting like a magnet, the hope of fresh meat driving them on. Sooner or later they would find a way in, gnawing through the flimsy walls, and death would be violent and painful. He shuddered at the thought and considered taking his own life before those gleaming teeth sank into his flesh. Until such time, however, he would do all he could to survive. For survive he must. So much money. So much to live for. He closed his eyes and wished for sleep to envelop him. The terror, however, refused to release its hold and he shivered and whimpered, waiting for the wolves to disperse.

Twenty eight

The previous day, as the women peered out over the top of the door and grew excited at whatever it was they saw, Shelby took his chance and slipped upstairs. He calculated he had less than five minutes. His first act was to visit Josh, lying in a bed, with the covers up to his chin. He looked like shit, his eyes red rimmed, skin the colour of a tallow candle. Reaching out his hand, Shelby touched his former partner's forehead and instantly recoiled. The flesh was clammy and cold. A quick glance towards the door and Shelby pulled out the metal embossed hip flask he always carried, uncorking it. Tipping it against Josh's lips, he allowed some of the whisky to dribble across the young man's lips. With a start, Josh's eyes sprang open and he spluttered, head snapping from side to side.

"Jesus, Shelby, what the fuck—"

Pleased to see some colour returning to the young man's cheeks, Shelby stooped down beside him. "Shut up, Josh, old friend, I haven't got much time."

"What do you mean, not much time? What's going on, Shelby? That damned woman shot me, I remember that and then they—"

"They're planning on hanging us, I know that much. I heard 'em. Can you?" He paused, hand held upright and, sure enough, the baying and jeering of a fast approaching mob of townsfolk came to them from out in the street. "The whole damned town is coming to lynch us from the telegraph pole, just like we did that bastard Sinclair."

"Oh good God Almighty, Shelby." A stick-thin hand crawled out from beneath the sheets to grip Shelby's arm. "What are we to do?"

"I'm going to get Clifton. Where did he go, old friend?"

"Oh shit, Shelby, you'll never find him! Due west is what he said, but I have no idea where due west is and nor did he. We was like blind men in the dark, Shelby. When we came upon the cabin, it was more through luck than design." He coughed, a deep rumbling sound, which brought tears to his eyes. "Give me some more of that whisky."

Shelby did so, chewing away at the inside of his cheek, thinking, trying to find some hope in Josh's words. "All right, due west. I have to try, Shelby. A cabin you say?"

"There's a trail, skirting the woods. Don't go into the woods too far, Shelby, they'll swallow you up whole. And there's Bannocks out there. Jesus, Shelby, you'll never make it."

"I have to try. When I find Clifton, I'll come back and we'll take over again. Now," he turned and looked around the room. "I need some clothing and a gun. Have you got yours, Josh?"

"I think it's over on that dresser, under the window. But, Shelby, for God's sake, if you get lost, you'll die out there. Think about it, please."

"If I stay here, Josh, I'm dead anyway."

"And me? Jesus, you gonna leave me here like this? What's to stop them hanging me once you've gone?"

"You tell them I've gone to get the rest of the gang, you understand?" Josh nodded. "Tell them we have an army out there, just waiting for my signal. And when we come back, we'll kill every last one of those miserable bastards if they dare to even touch you. You understand?" Another nod. "All right, Josh, old friend, you hang on in and all will be well. I give you my word."

In a mad flurry, Shelby ran over to the dresser and took up Josh's gun, checking it first before stuffing it into his waistband. He pulled on a thick overcoat, which proved a little too small for him. Unable to button it up fully, he took a shawl draped over the back of wicker-backed chair and tied it around his neck. A faint whiff of lavender rose up to his nostrils and he grimaced before moving to the side of the window and lifting the sash. A blast of cold air blew in and he recoiled for a moment.

"Take this, Shelby," said Josh, his voice fracturing as he sat up and strained to grab hold of his floppy, wide-brimmed hat.

Shelby crossed the room and took it, Josh collapsing back amongst the bed-clothes. He let out a rattling breath. "Damn it, Shelby, you'd best be quick. I'm not sure if I can last."

"You better. If you think I'm going out in that snow for nothing …" He forced a laugh and Josh smiled. Gripping the boy by the shoulder, Shelby swung around and, with raised voices growing angry from below, he slid out through the window and inched his way along the ledge.

Twenty nine

The girl rode alongside him, Curly grumbling and groaning some half a dozen paces behind as Simms set a steady pace across the plain towards the town of Glory. The trail took a winding course, often hidden beneath the snow, but Simms had the advantage of his old army compass, which he referred to often, checking the direction.

"What is that thing you're forever looking at?" asked Tabatha when Simms snapped the lid of the tiny contraption shut for the umpteenth time that morning.

"I got it from an old friend of mine, half a lifetime ago. Never had much need to use it until now, what with all of this snow."

"It tells you which direction to head for?"

"If you can read it, yes. See this here needle," he pulled it from his pocket again and opened the lid. She drew her horse closer and strained to see, "it always points north, so if you fix your bearings, you will head the correct way. It works in fog, rain, wind or snow. Even at night."

"How does it do that?"

Simms smiled. "I have no idea, I just know it works. Saved my life a few times back in the War, but that's another story."

He caught her look, felt the heat rise to his cheeks and turned away, slipping the compass back into his coat.

"You must have been angry when you saw what Annabelle and Lamont did."

Simms grunted, rolling his shoulders, feeling the discomfort seeping up between his shoulder blades. The intensity of her look unsettled him, not that he minded the closeness of her body too much, but confusion gnawed away at him. Her relationship with Curly seemed strange. They showed little affection towards each other, almost as if they were brother and sister rather than lovers. But hadn't Annabelle told him that they were engaged to be married? Perhaps he'd heard wrong, perhaps he'd misunderstood. Her eyes, however, told a very different story, eyes which penetrated into his very soul. Warm eyes, nevertheless. Not ones easily resisted, even if he wanted to. Surrendering to her searching gaze, heart swelling and a lump developing in his throat, he smiled at her. "I'd be lying if I said I didn't want to kill them both, right there. The Bannocks, they sort of changed the situation."

"And you killed them."

"I had to. I've learned it's best not to parley with those who are intent on taking your head off your shoulders."

Nodding, her eyes wandered across the frozen plain. "I sometimes wish we had never left Kansas. I do not believe any of us ever imagined how hard the journey across to California would be."

"No one ever does."

"But you made it," she turned again, studying him. "You've made a life for yourself out here."

A sudden image of Noreen rose up in his mind and he bit down on his lip, lowered his head and concentrated on his gloved hands gripping the reins. "It hasn't been easy."

"Oh? Why, what has happened?"

"Too much." He pulled in a deep breath and pointed to a large outcrop of rocks some distance away. "We can shelter over there. We'll make a fire, eat what we can. Although the snow has stopped, the temperature will continue to fall as daylight recedes. We'll need to get something hot inside us if we're to make Glory before nightfall."

Without a word, her hand reached out and rested on his arm. He shot his eyes to her fingers as if he'd been scalded.

"You should talk about it."

"I don't think that would be such a good idea." He felt her grip tighten, but he didn't pull away, liking the sensation her touch brought. "I just do my job is all."

"There's a lot of pain in your eyes, Detective. I can see it."

Not knowing what to say, he managed a feeble, "Oh," and checked his compass again for something to do. As her hand slipped away, a wave of disappointment came over him. He tried his best to ignore it but failed miserably. As they crossed the plain towards the rocks, he found himself checking to make sure she continued ambling close by and when she caught him looking, he blushed again. And Tabatha giggled.

It was a welcome sound in that harsh place.

* * *

Across the sky, great bands of purple and orange competed for supremacy whilst the wind howled and snow flurries swept through the empty street. Hunched up in their coats, hats pulled down, scarves covering mouths, the three riders inched forward in silence. Nobody ventured out to greet them, or even fire a questioning glance. At the sheriff's office, Simms got down from the saddle and stretched his back before looping the reins around the hitching rail. Stomping his feet on the boardwalk he nodded over to Curly and Tabatha, both sitting on their horses, noses red, breath steaming. "I'll check in with the sheriff. Then we can see about finding ourselves somewhere warm and dry to rest."

Without waiting for any reply, Simms put his gloved hand on the door handle and pushed it. It was locked and he stepped over to the window adjacent and, cupping his face against the glass, tried to peer inside.

"Sheriff ain't there, son."

Simms turned and frowned at the short, elderly man standing a few paces from him, swathed in a voluminous fur coat of great age and even greater smell. Wrinkling his nose, Simms said, "And where might I find him?"

"In the cemetery." The old man cackled at Simms's perplexed look. "Yessir, that's what I said. Went and got himself shot. I saw it. Every moment of it. Darnedest thing I ever did see, that's the living truth of it."

"I didn't quite catch your name, old-timer."

"Well, *old-timer* it ain't, sonny. My name is Dempsey. That's what they call me and that's who I am. And like I said, I saw 'em shoot Dylan Forbes dead, I did. I stood next to him in the street, with his body blown apart and his eyes rolling." He leaned forward, "You fixing on stayin' here a while? Best not be going to the Golden Nugget. That's where they is at."

"Who?"

"Why everyone! Didn't you notice how quiet it all is?" He cackled again and turned his face to the others, his eyes widening as he singled out Tabatha for extra attention. "My, my, you is a pretty young thing, but you is looking mighty cold. My advice would be—"

"The men who killed the sheriff," put in Simms quickly, "they are still here?"

"Far as I know. Like I say, over at the Golden Nugget, that's where they all is. The Mayor and Mr Springer. Saw them all coming in with a bunch of folk. No doubt they'll be having a meeting about what to do."

Simms looked across to the others. "We'll go and take a look, after we've stabled the horses. Tabatha, don't go wandering off none. This place strikes me as a mite unfriendly."

"Oh, it surely is," said Dempsey, enjoying the expressions of fear crossing the young peoples' faces. "Livery stable is over yonder," he pointed a gnarled finger to a cluster of large buildings on the opposite side of the broad street. "There won't be no one there, but for a dollar or two I'll take your horses over there for you."

With a grunt Simms fished out a silver dollar and placed it into the old man's palm. "Unsaddle and feed them, if you would. I'll come along and check on them after I've spoke to this – who did you say the mayor was?"

"Mr Howard, but he has no more say in this place than I have. Springer is the man to speak to."

"I understand a US Marshal has been sent for?"

"Well," the finger appeared again, this time pointing towards a side street over to the right, "we did have a telegraph office, with one them new-fangled telegraphic contraptions, but one of them boys who killed Dylan blew all the lines down with his six-gun. Dandiest bit of shooting I ever did see."

Pursing his lips, Simms automatically reached inside his coat and patted the handle of his Colt Dragoon. He then nodded across to Curly. "If this gets hairy, you get the hell out and take Tabatha with you."

"I ain't going anywhere without you, Detective," said the girl. "You give me a gun and I'll cover you. Curly will go round the back, if you give him your carbine."

Tilting his head, Simms narrowed one eye, "If either of you cross me—"

"Please don't insult me," she said. "We've come this far together and I've made you a promise to come back with you to Bovey and give witness. I don't go back on my word, Detective."

After a few moments, Simms let out a long breath, reaching under his armpit and drawing out the Navy Colt. He stepped down and gave it to her, butt first said, "It has five shots loaded. Make sure you make every last one count."

Hefting it in her hand, she slipped the revolver under her belt and smiled. "And then perhaps we might find a fire and a good bowl of hot soup."

"I'll second that," said Curly.

Simms went to his horse and pulled out his carbine. He handed it over to the young man who took it with something akin to reverence.

"One shot," said Simms and stepped away. "I'm putting my trust in you both. If any shooting breaks out, we do what we can. Don't think twice."

"Hot God Almighty," piped up Old Man Dempsey, doing a little jig, "I do declare justice has returned to these here streets."

"Well, let's hope we're still here to talk about it afterwards." Simms doffed his hat and strode down the boardwalk towards the Golden Nugget saloon.

Thirty

He saw the trails of smoke rising up from the buildings long before he realised he had wandered way off course. As he urged his horse, or rather the horse he had stolen after dropping down from the saloon window, to the top of a rise, he peered out over the stunning white landscape and sighed. In the distance nestled a spread of buildings, a single street bisecting them. A larger building, which he assumed was a church, stood at the far end but nothing of any further merit took his interest. Another anonymous town struggling to survive after the gold and silver mines petered out. Forlorn, clinging on in the hope of better days to come but no doubt almost virtually deserted, the population long since gone. Perhaps it was better that way, at least for now. At least for Shelby. He pulled the scarf tighter around his throat and moved on.

Entering the street, he noted a flat wagon, with a pair of horse in front, parked outside a dull, tired looking saloon. He decided to head for it. Nothing else stirred in that soulless place so he reined in his horse and went inside, shaking himself.

The bar room was large and dimly lit. A fire spluttered over on the right and he headed straight for it, ignoring the two men at the bar and the barman behind the counter. Aware of their presence and their curious looks, he bade them no mind, desperate for warmth. A large black-spotted dog lay sprawled in front of the flames and opened one eye to consider Shelby for a moment before settling back into sleep.

"Cold, ain't it," muttered someone over at the counter.

Shelby, hands stretched out before the flames, lost in the bliss of warmth, managed a grunt in return.

"You have whisky?" he asked, eyes closed, breathing in the thick air. He could stay here, make a life, never venture outside again.

"If you have the money to pay for one."

Patting his pocket, he nodded, "Have no fear, I can pay my way." He remained with his back to the men until he heard the reassuring trickle of alcohol filling up a glass. Only then did he swagger across the room, take up the whisky and down it in one. Eyes closed, he held his breath, allowing the fiery liquid to settle in his stomach and almost immediately felt human again. "Like you said, it's cold."

"You came across the plain?" asked one of the men. "From Glory?"

"I was looking for a friend of mine. Name of Dylan Forbes, Sheriff of said Glory. I understood he had a place, but I missed it, probably by miles."

"Don't know him," shrugged the speaker, casting a quick glance to the man next to him, who repeated the shrug. He then turned to the barman. "How about you, Clinton?"

Clinton filled up Shelby's whisky glass without waiting to be asked. "I know him. Or should I say, I know his woman." He pushed over the glass. "What's your interest, friend?"

"I have a message for him. It's kinda personal." Shelby picked up the glass and studied it. "His woman, you say? I guess I could give her the message and she could pass it on."

"Seems sensible." Clinton put his hands on the counter rim and pushed himself backwards. "Problem is, she came through here a few days ago and she ain't come back – least not this way. In this weather, anything could have happened."

"Indians," said the first man, shaking his head. "Damned Indians everywhere. Starving they are and they will take anything you have, including your scalp, if you come across 'em. We had a scrape with them ourselves, didn't we Harry?"

"We sure did," said Harry with feeling.

"Barely got out alive," continued the other as he lifted his own drink and took a sip. "We won't be venturing westwards again, not until this weather lifts and we can see where we're going."

"You say you missed their cabin," said Clinton, ignoring the others, his eyes regarding Shelby with a keen interest. Shelby nodded and took a drink, swilling the whisky around his mouth before swallowing it and gasping with relish. "Well, it's easy to find. Just head back towards Glory and when you come across the first woodland you see, it's right there."

"I need to rest first. Thaw out my bones."

"I see. Well, what I don't understand is, if you couldn't find the cabin, how come you made it here?"

"Saw the smoke from the chimneys," said Shelby and finished his whisky. "Listen, I'd love to talk some more, but I need a room and a hot meal."

"We ain't got no rooms."

The air grew chiller than that outside. Harry and his friend exchanged a look.

"You don't seem especially busy," said Shelby, his voice low, eyes averted.

"We're full."

"Clinton," said the first man, "this man is frozen through, surely you've—"

"I *said*, we're full." Clinton puffed out his chest. "Take the road out of town, mister. Head towards the mountains. You'll come to a homestead before you reach them and I'm sure the folk there will offer you a room for the night."

Shelby gave himself a moment before he brought his face up to meet Clinton's furious glare. "I'm not sure why you're taken such a dislike to me, Clinton, but, I have to say, it does upset me. Now, I'm gonna ask you again and this time I'd be obliged if you consider my request with a good deal more alacrity and give an answer which is far more acceptable. I want a room."

"We ain't got one. And," Clinton came forward again, his teeth clenched, eyes narrowed, "I'll be asking you to pay for your drinks before you get on out. Five dollars."

"Kiss my ass, Clinton."

"I know your kind. I spoke to Hanson about it and he warned me there might be someone coming here, asking questions."

"Hanson? I don't know anybody called Hanson." Shelby turned a quizzical look towards the others, both of whom did their usual shrug of unknowing. "So tell me who the hell he is and how he knows me."

"I didn't say he knows *you*, just your kind. He said someone might come, asking about the woman and, if they came, then I was to point them in the direction of the place I mentioned. Now get the hell out of here, mister, before I forget my manners."

His hands reached below the counter and re-emerged less than a second later with a sawn off, twin-barrelled shotgun. As he brought it round to bear on Shelby, the other two men instinctively stepped away, aware of how such a weapon, once discharged, delivered a fearsome, uncontrolled spread.

But they did need to worry. Not about the shotgun.

Shelby's hand came up in a blur and he shot Clinton between the eyes. A look of abject amazement crossed the barman's features before he pitched backwards and smashed against the stack of bottles and glasses on the shelves behind him. Without pausing to admire his handiwork, Shelby turned and plugged the other two in the guts, Harry receiving an extra bullet in the neck as he crumpled to the floor. Stepping across the corpse, Shelby got down next to the other, who squirmed and squealed, trying desperately to stem the flow of blood spewing from the wound in his stomach. Shelby reached inside the man's coat and deftly relieved him of the firearm he had spotted in the holster high up on the man's hip. Grinning, he went over to the counter again and helped himself to another measure of whisky. Below, the man groaned, right hand reaching out, begging.

Shelby shot him through the head and, as the cordite drifted listlessly towards the ceiling, the silence settled over the room once more, this time a lot less chilly than previously.

Partaking of yet another whisky, Shelby retired to the fire. He frowned. The dog, which appeared comatose last time he saw it, was gone. Unconcerned, he flopped down into a nearby chair, cradling the glass in his lap, stretching out his booted feet towards the fire. He really should pull them off, dry out his socks, restore his strength before setting off again. H decided to head back the way he came, but try a slightly different direction, seek out the wood Clinton mentioned.

Satisfied with this plan, he settled himself back in the chair and closed his eyes. In a little while, he'd retire upstairs, find a comfortable room and get some rest. Perhaps later, rustle himself up some food, a little more whisky … A smile of utter contentment spread across his face as, without opening his eyes, he drained his glass and cleared his mind of thoughts.

The swing doors burst open and a herd of heavy feet and angry voices came pouring in from the cold. Shelby opened one eye and peered towards this intrusion with barely contained annoyance.

Crowding around him, pointing their various firearms with clear intention, the intruders appeared jittery and angry in equal proportions and Shelby shelved any ideas of shooting his way out of the situation.

For the time being.

Thirty one

Approaching the entrance, placing his feet as lightly as possible, the raised voices from within grew in intensity with every step. Taking a breath, he glanced over his shoulder to see Tabatha close behind, gun in hand. She gave him a reassuring smile as Curly sprinted past, disappearing around the nearest corner, presumably to take up his position at the rear. Simms released his breath in a steady, smoking stream and burst through the doors.

The scene confronting him was one of pure confusion. People were shouting, gesticulating, waggling fingers and demanding answers. In the centre of this large press of townsfolk, two men were doing their ablest to calm everyone down but nobody seemed prepared to listen. Certainly none of them noticed Simms's entrance so he stood and waited whilst Tabatha stepped up beside him and sighed. "They seem awful mad. Wonder what's irked them so."

Before he could offer an explanation, no matter how off-beam, a young, full-breasted woman dressed in an impossibly tight dress, hitched up her tresses and climbed onto a table. She raised her hand, filled with a large revolver, aimed the barrel to the ceiling and loosed off a single shot. The subsequent boom sounded unnaturally loud in that thick, unwholesome air, but had the desired effect as every eye snapped towards her and silence fell.

"God damn you all, stop with the jabbering! We need to work out what to do when Shelby gets back with all of his men, instead of talking about who did what and when. Wake up and arm up, because when he comes, he'll bring hell with him."

Faced with a sea of incredulous and frightened faces, the woman went to jump down when she caught sight of Simms and Tabatha and her body froze. In a low, fearful voice, she said, "Or maybe hell has already come a-calling."

Taking her lead, individuals turned to see of whom she spoke. A few gasps followed but nobody made any move towards a gun. Perplexed, the crowd waited and the seconds crawled by until, at last, one of the two men in the centre pushed his way through the others, straightening himself up to his full height, doing his best to appear resolute. "Are you part of the gang, sir? Because if you are, you need to know that we will not—"

"We're part of no gang," drawled Simms and slipped the Dragoon back into the holster. "I'm Detective Simms from the Pinkerton Detective Agency and I need you to tell me what in the name of God is going on here."

* * *

Sitting at a table close to the fire, the three of them finished off their plates of eggs and grits, washing down the food with plenty of hot coffee. From a nearby table, the woman in the tight-fitting bodice regarded them with silent curiosity whilst beside her the spokesman of the now dispersed townspeople cleared his throat and said, "My name is Norton Springer. Over by the bar is the town mayor, Gerald Howard. Beside him is acting alderman, Mrs Mary Hubert. We are all that is left of the town council, the rest having been murdered by that blackheart called Shelby. If you would allow me, sir, I will give you the details of what has befallen our once peaceful and law-abiding community."

Simms looked across at Tabatha. Beside her Curly ran a piece of bread around the rim of his plate, disinterested in anything else but finishing his meal. The girl, on the other hand, had eyes only for the detective. Glancing away, he felt the heat rising to his jaw line again. Every time she looked his way, the same thing happened. He wondered what power she possessed, this mysterious ability to transform him into a weak, bemused little—

"Sir? If I may be so bold, can you tell us what your plan is?"

Simms blinked, dragging himself out of his reverie and caught Springer's intensely serious expression. "My plan? Well, from what I hear, you have sent for a US Marshal, who shall be arriving from Bridger as soon as this weather clears. I have been asked to assess the situation here and act accordingly."

"We sent for a marshal some weeks ago, when Judge Malpas was found shot dead in his office. However things have developed since then and we sent a subsequent message. Is it your intention to wait here until the marshal comes?"

"I didn't say that. I have my own business awaiting me back at Bovey. I need to be back there by tomorrow." Again his eyes fell on Tabatha. "I might already be too late."

"But you can't just go and leave us," blurted out the woman at the bar and she strode across the room to stand, hands on hips, glaring down at the detective. "You're a law officer. We need your protection."

"Ma'am, you have enough guns around here to hold down an army of Comanches. You don't need me."

"Yes we do," she insisted, her eyes flashing. "You have no idea what kind of man he is – what he is capable of."

"Oh, I think I can guess."

"Then it is your duty to apprehend him."

Simms sat back in his chair and folded his arms. "Ma'am, may I make a suggestion?" For a moment her eyes softened and she shot a look towards Springer, who leaned forward, interested. "Why not swear Curly here in as town sheriff. He will then have the authority to swear in deputies, which will make everything legal. He can arrest this ..." He frowned towards the woman in the bodice. "What did you say his name was?"

"Shelby," she said.

"Yeah, well ... This *Shelby*, once thrown into a cell, will sit there and wait for the marshal to arrive."

Across the table Curly at last stirred, pushing his plate away. He ran his tongue across his teeth, taking his time to enjoy the remnants of his meal. "Detective, ain't you forgetting something?"

"Am I? What?"

"*Me.* I have no intention of becoming no sheriff, not for this flea-ridden hole, or anywhere else for that matter."

"You'll do as you're told son," said Simms, his voice taking on a dangerous tone, "or I'll make sure you stand trial along with your mother back at Bovey."

"She ain't my mother."

"Nevertheless."

Leaning across, Tabatha squeezed Curly's arm. "It's best you do what he says. We can make everything right again, Curly. Once we're free of this, there's always California to consider."

Biting down on his bottom lip, Curly dropped his head. "I didn't think you still wanted to go."

"We'll see how it all pans out, Curly. A lot of things have changed. It's time to make it all better again."

For a moment, Curly appeared to struggle with himself, chewing feverishly at his mouth, breathing growing erratic. Finally, his face red and eyes glazed, he stared straight into Simms's eyes. "Damn you for coming across us that day."

"It's a good job he did," interjected Tabatha.

Curly tore his arm free of her. "And damn you, for all the lies you spout!"

"People," said Springer, "I'm not sure what is going on here, but if you think this young man is up to the job, then I for one agree. What about you, Gerald?"

The mayor grunted, went to speak, but finally nodded. Mrs Hubert blew out a breath. "Shelby is like no one else I've ever seen. He is violent and unpredictable."

"And a drunk," said the girl. "If he's drunk he's as worthless as a dead match in a dark room. I'll get him drunk, then we can overpower him."

"You'll do that for us, Stella?" asked Springer.

She nodded. "If the pay is right, I'll do anything you Goddamn please."

Mrs Hubert hissed. "At least you're loyal to your profession. Very well, it's agreed. Can you swear this man in, Detective?"

"Nope," he jabbed a finger towards Howard, "that'll have to be you, Mr Mayor. I'll get back to Bovey and send off another telegram to Bridger. In the meantime, you arm up, position your best shots in strategic places around town and keep a careful watch on the trail. If what you tell me is true, and Shelby has got more men, you're going to need every ounce of courage to get you through. I shall return in a couple more days, once I've completed my duties. For now," he stood up and pulled on his coat, "I'm going to have a few words with the fella you have upstairs. You can join me, if you have a mind to, miss...?"

The girl smiled. "My name's Stella."

"And me," put in Tabatha quickly.

"You don't need to come," said Simms.

"I know," she said, "but I'm going to." Together, the three climbed the stairs, leaving Curly to sit and stare at his empty plate.

* * *

They found Josh propped up in bed, dozing, his head lolling on his chest. As the door opened, he jerked upright, surprise giving away swiftly to joy as he saw Stella moving towards him.

"How you feeling," she said, stooping down beside the bed. She brushed his forehead with the back of her hand and his eyes closed for a moment.

"Much better now you're here."

Behind her, Simms coughed and Stella, chuckling, moved away to allow the two men to consider one another.

"I need you to tell me what you know of this Shelby fella," said Simms.

Stella quickly interjected, "Josh, this man is what they call a detective. A lawman, I guess. He's here to help."

"I'm a Pinkerton Detective," said Simms, "hailing from Illinois, but stationed at Bovey. My jurisdiction is limited, but I have some influence. I'm guessing that is what might interest you, if we made some kind of deal?"

"I've done some bad things, mister. If you can put a word in for me, I'd be obliged."

"If you tell me what Shelby wants from this town, what brought him here and why he may return, then I give you my word the court will go easy on you – if, indeed, you ever get to court. Often things have a way of sorting themselves out, if you understand my meaning."

"Yes, I believe I do. If you have a little time, I'll tell you all you need to know."

Nodding, Simms sat down on the bed and listened to the story of Shelby, Lance Sinclair, the double-cross and Shelby's desire to get back the money he believed to be his. By the time the story was ended, Simms believed he had a fairly good idea of who he might have to go up against. He also suspected that his hopes for the townspeople taking care of things for themselves might be a little misplaced.

Downstairs again, Simms stopped at the last step and smiled as he witnessed Gerald Howard in the act of pinning a sheriff's badge on Curly's shirt. The young man looked down at it and touched one of the points of the metal star.

"Everything will be just fine, Curly," said Tabatha, stepping up beside him to rub his arm.

"I don't think things will ever be fine again. The chips are down, Tabby, and the cards all played out."

"Don't say such things, Curly."

He looked over her shoulder to Simms and sighed. "But you're playing a different game now, I can see that."

She gave a little gasp but before she could say anything Springer stepped up and took Curly by the arm. "Come on, I'll show you to your office. It'll need something of a sweep out, but I think you'll find it a respectable little place from which to do business. Detective Simms, if you'll take my advice, you'll stay here for the night and set off for Bovey at first light. You'll never make it before dark if you set off now, and I would not wish to be out on the plains at night."

Simms allowed his shoulders to drop. "I reckon you're right."

Doffing his hat, Springer turned away and, together with Curly, tramped out of the saloon, the bat-doors swinging noisily on their hinges. People slowly drifted away, some lingering at the bar to take a drink. Howard exchanged words with Mrs Hubert before they nodded their farewells to Simms and left. With Stella remaining upstairs with Josh, Simms found himself virtually alone with Tabatha for the first time since they came across one another that morning back at the abandoned hotel. She smiled up at him. "You think they can handle him?"

"Shelby?" She nodded. "I hope so. It'll take us a day to get back to Bovey, another day to present my evidence to the sheriff and the circuit judge then another to get back here. Three days. Everything depends on where Shelby is and if he decides to come back."

"I think he will."

"Oh? What makes you so certain?"

"Stella. She's a fine looking woman and she obviously knows him well, if you get my drift."

"If you're talking about affection, then from what I've seen most of hers is centred on Josh."

"Yes, but she's a whore – she can play her part well. I reckon Shelby thinks he can make a new woman of her." Her smile broadened and she stepped up close, so close he could smell her perfume. She laughed as he wrinkled his nose. "I borrowed some of Stella's French Cologne. You like it?"

His throat grew tight and he went to step away, but she took him by the lapels and forced him to her. He gulped. "Tabatha, I don't think—"

"Don't think. That's your problem, you think too damned much."

He glanced across to the bar, catching the amused expressions of some of the men standing there and blowing out his cheeks. "Jeez, Tabatha, you can't just—"

"Yes I can," she said, dropping her hands, releasing him only for a moment before she took hold of his hand and steered him up the staircase, "and what's more, I'm going to."

Thirty two

Muffled by the snow, the noise of the flat bottomed wagon was barely audible as Shelby steered it out of the town, but curious onlookers still came out and watched him move by. He paid them little attention, knowing there would be no posse sent after him. Riverneck was a dead town, its death rattle echoing through the miserable streets and the broken, creaking buildings. Soon it would fall into abandonment, like so many old mining towns, and become just another footnote in the history of the American West.

The men had stood in a tight circle, their ancient, rusted firearms shaking in grips made weak with fear. There were five of them, all the worst part of sixty. He smiled and stood up, the guns in his hands coming up, and shot them, one by one, his laughter ringing out louder than the blasts. Afterwards, he found a room and stretched himself out, a whisky bottle for company, and fell into a blissful, untroubled sleep.

The town became nothing but a bad memory as he headed east, head down against the wind. Keeping the tree line close to his left, he followed the advice of those he had so recently murdered. Like everything else, he paid them little mind. All of his thoughts were centred on one thing and one thing alone. To find Sinclair's woman and take back the money. So he let the nag set its own pace and he dozed, huddled against the cold. At least the snow had stopped and the occasional flash of blue sky gave the promise of better weather to come.

He stopped more than once to jump down from his seat and pound his boots into the ground, beating his body with his own arms, desperate for warmth. At such times he would uncork his hip flask and drink down the brandy he had purloined from the saloon. Senses swayed, eyes grew blurry, but he did not care. When at last the trees separated into two, sprawling woods, the little cabin appeared alongside the track. When he saw it, he pulled back hard on the reins and stared.

Nothing stirred.

The cabin stood forlorn, its roof sagging in the centre, steps and porch splintered, slats broken. Shelby's breath steamed from his mouth as he struggled to keep himself calm. All around the little wooden house were the tell-tale signs of a life and death struggle, with large patches of pink hyphenating the snowy ground. And a horse, its guts ripped out, the remnants of its innards like thick, pink ropes thrown out around the frozen carcass.

He clambered down from the seat. The nag snorted, eyes wide with alarm, so he slowly led it back a little and tied the rein around a nearby tree. Something spooked the animal and was spooking Shelby even more. Drawing his revolver, he took his time and advanced, eyes alert, breathing through his open mouth, listening out for the merest sound.

Pressing his ear to the door, he could discern no sound from within. He took a moment and looked towards the nearby trees. There was a carcass there, between two spindly trunks. A wolf, long dead, frozen solid. Close to starving in this bleak land, the wolves must have come upon the cabin in the hope of finding food. They found the horse, perhaps fought amongst themselves for the choicest morsels. But why would a horse be here, alone? He shivered, pulled his coat tight around his throat and put his shoulder to the door.

It barely moved, the timbers swollen with the cold or perhaps with something else. Groaning, he gritted his teeth, tried again, all of his strength straining against the wood. Inch by inch the door gave way, gradually opening enough to reveal nothing but blackness and –

"Arh, dear God Almighty," he said aloud, retreating, hand clamped over his nose and mouth, the stench causing his stomach to lurch. He bent double and vomited, the bile burning his throat, the sound ringing out, penetrating the trees. Any hope of remaining quiet or maintaining the advantage of surprise all gone. He hacked and coughed and spat into the ground. Gasping, he took out his hip flask and drank down a large swig of brandy. Leaning against the doorframe, he waited for the waves of nausea to pass and the stench of decay to leave his nostrils.

He pushed through the gap, blinking to allow his eyes to adjust to the gloom. Propped against the door sat a man, stone dead, his skin a ghastly light grey pallor. Over to the left, another body, barely recognisable, with two wolves lying across it. All dead. Shelby sucked in a breath, glancing again at the man at the door. His throat was open, black frozen blood cascading down across his chest. In his lap the stumps of his arms, gnawed through by ravenous mouths, and a gun with another still in its holster. Shelby took this one, checked it and found it fully primed. He put it in his waistband and narrowed his eyes.

In the far end of the room was something else.

Saddlebags.

With barely contained glee, he ran over to them and pulled open the flaps and what he saw made everything worthwhile and the world a wonderful place once more. Money. Bundles of bank-notes and heaps of gold coins. Sinclair's horde.

Shelby looked across to the dead man again and wondered who he might have been. Had Sinclair's woman found herself a better offer? He didn't know, didn't care; his only thought that he was now rich. Stella would be his. She wouldn't think twice. The thought of her slim, nubile thighs gripping him as he screamed his way through their coupling brought a sudden urgency to his loins. He ran outside like a little boy, skipping and laughing as he went. He threw the stuffed saddlebags into the back of the flat wagon and, with the cold all forgotten, flicked the reins across the old nag's back and made his way along the winding track back to Glory and the certain hope of love and the beginning of a new life, one worth living.

Thirty three

"Don't worry, please. Honestly, it doesn't matter. Really."

He stood staring out of the window and she was behind him, head resting on his shoulder, arms curled around his waist. Her words sounded flat; he didn't believe them. And her arms, going through the motions, holding him because it was the right thing to do, to comfort him, offer him support. Closing his eyes, desperate to wish it all away. Noreen. The mother of his child. Both of them dead.

Turning in her arms, he forced a smile before he pushed past her, took up his shirt hanging on the bedpost and dragged it on. From the window she folded her arms, mouth down turned slightly.

"It's not you," he said, not wanting to get into a debate about why he couldn't make love to her, but realising she needed some sort of explanation. "My wife …"

Tabatha cocked her head. "I didn't know you were married. You never said."

"No," he fumbled with the buttons, "I haven't any more. She died, you see. Giving birth to our – to our only child."

She crossed the few steps to him at a rush, cupping his face in his hands and kissing him lightly on the lips. "I'm so sorry – you should have said."

He shrugged and, before he knew what was happening, she was helping him close up the buttons on his shirt. He watched her slim fingers and wished he was anybody else in any other world but this.

Awkwardness was nothing unusual for Simms, especially when around women. All of his usual assertiveness and confidence drained away in their presence. He knew of no way to stop it. So he fidgeted and forced a grin, knowing he looked apish and slightly comical, but what could he do? Tabatha's eyes swallowed him up whole. He realised in any other situation he would gladly surrender to her charms, but his grief ate away at him and, no matter how he tried, Noreen's face came to him. Such a lovely face. The only woman for whom he had shown any kind of affection. If things were somehow different, who knows … But they could never be. Unless Tabatha's patience was infinite, but he knew he could never expect such a thing from her. Young and vibrant, she could have anyone she wished. For one fleeting moment, she had chosen him and he had failed her. So he muttered his apologies, strapped his gun around his waist and went out, afraid to catch her eyes.

Thankfully, most of the revellers from earlier had long since wandered away. A few remained, one of them being Springer, holding court by the bar with a trio of indignant looking men in wide brimmed hats and portly bellies, all bobbing heads and quaffing drinks. They stopped as Simms came down the stairs, dragging on his coat. Springer arched a single eyebrow.

"You care to join us, Detective?"

Simms flashed a warning glance across the men, all of whom averted their eyes. They may not know the details of what had occurred upstairs, but he knew what lurked behind their mocking leers.

"I need to make my way back to Bovey," he said.

They men shared a look of abject horror. Springer stepped forward, "But you can't – what if he comes back?"

"You have Curly and his deputies. The rest of you, as I say, position yourselves around town, keep a lookout. If he comes, you fire warning shots, then you do what you need to. I shall return in two days."

"But what if you don't," said one of the men. "What if something happens to delay you?"

"Like I say, you deal with it."

"And if he starts shooting?"

"You shoot back. Listen, I'm not your nursemaid. You do what is necessary. Trust in Curly – I do."

Over in the far corner, a chair scraped over the wooden floorboards and Simms turned to see Mrs Hubert. Her eyes appeared glazed, something which took him by surprise. He never would have taken her for a drinker and yet there she was, swaying slightly, her mouth slack. "Detective, I shall ensure every man does his duty."

Grunting, Simms adjusted his coat and paused as Tabatha came down the stairs to join him. She looked handsome in a black serge coat buttoned to the throat, black hat pulled right down over her brows. Around her waist, a gun belt and in its holster, Simms's Navy Colt. If anything, it made her even more attractive than before.

"I'm accompanying Mr Simms," she said.

Springer nodded, "Ah-huh."

"What does that mean?"

Springer shrugged. "It means I'm thinking our dear detective here will be a mite longer than three days if he has you by his side."

Smiling, she stepped up close to the bank owner. "Jealous, are we?"

The others laughed and Springer's face developed a deep red glow, which only provoked further laughter from those close by. Flustered, he looked away and threw a glass of whisky down his throat. "Just make sure you get back here pronto."

Turning on his heels, Simms strode out of the Golden Nugget without comment. Tabatha quickly followed and, smiling up at him, slipped her hand in his. He didn't pull away.

Thirty four

Martinson jumped up with a start as the door crashed open, cracking his knee on the desk edge. He cried out and bent over, vigorously rubbing the injury with both hands.

"If you're that nervous," drawled Sheriff Miller as he stepped inside, "you should have locked the door."

"Ah, damn that," said Martinson, grimacing. He sucked in air through his teeth and flopped back into his chair. "I've been up all night with that damn woman singing her hymns."

"I don't hear nothin'."

"That's because she's stopped now and fallen asleep, goddamn her."

Chuckling to himself, Miller strode over to the cell and peered through the bars. Annabelle lay huddled on the narrow single bunk set against the far wall. A threadbare blanket barely covered her and one naked leg hung out to trail onto the floor. Miller sighed. "She's a mighty handsome woman. What did Simms say she did to cause him to arrest her?"

"He didn't."

"Well, that just about settles it." He turned and gave Martinson a long, penetrating look. "His time's up and so is hers. I'm letting her go, as per our agreement."

"Now hold on, you can't just—"

"I can do whatever I damn well please, storekeeper. This is my town, I make the rules. Simms said he'd return with the evidence and he has failed to do so."

Leaning forward across the desk, Martinson held his breath, measuring his words with great care. "From what I recall, you gave him five days."

"Yes, and that period ends today."

"My schooling tells me a day ends at midnight, Sheriff."

"Are you kidding me?"

"No. I'm just telling you as it is. Simms has until midnight."

"But I can't let her go in the middle of the night – where in the hell is she supposed to go?"

"Then let's say tomorrow morning. Nine o'clock. I'd call that fair, for all of us. For all we know, Simms could be about to come back into town even as we speak."

"And for all we know, he might be lying out on the prairie with his throat cut and his body used as a pincushion by Utes."

"Highly unlikely."

"But possible." Miller's shoulders relaxed. "All right, let's say nine o'clock. But as soon as that church bell sounds off, I'm walking in here to set her loose."

Martinson nodded, his breath released in a long, low stream. "You're nothing but fair, Sheriff."

"And you're nothing but a vessel full of horse-shit. I'll see you tomorrow."

He stormed out, slamming the door with such force the tiny jailhouse shuddered.

From her bunk, Annabelle groaned, turned onto her back and stretched out her body. Martinson tried his best not to look, but failed, her lithe body drawing him in. She sat up, her white slip falling from her shoulder, a honey-coloured shoulder, the skin smooth, unblemished. Martinson swallowed hard and caught her smiling eyes. He looked away.

"I'd appreciate some coffee," she said, her eyes not leaving his.

With the heat rising to his jawline, Martinson stood up and crossed to the stove, grateful to be free from her gaze, if only for a few moments. He busied himself with the coffee whilst behind him, inside the cell, he heard her yawning, adjusting clothes, naked feet padding across the stone floor. He chanced a glance over his shoulder and didn't think he had ever seen a more beautiful woman.

"Make it strong," she said, her hands gripping the bars as she leaned as close as her prison allowed. "I like it strong. Like my men."

Snapping his face away, Martinson squeezed his eyes shut and tried to swallow again. How many years had it been since his wife died, taken with the fever? He tried to think, but with his mind filled with images of the glorious creature a matter of two paces away, he found any other thought difficult to conjure. His hand shook as he spooned ground coffee beans into the pot.

"I heard what the sheriff said," she continued. "Do you think the detective will return in time?"

Shrugging his shoulders, Martinson kept his concentration on making the coffee, pouring in the water from a stone jug and settling the pot on top of the stove. "I reckon he will do what he needs to do."

"You think he's still alive? I have heard terrible tales of what goes on out on the prairie. Indians, thieves and murderers."

"And other things." Martinson turned. Her thick raven hair fell to her bare shoulders, accentuating the glow of her fine skin. Without any conscious effort, his eyes dropped to the swell of her breasts, their milky softness pressing against the flimsy material of her slip.

"Other things?" She titled her head. "What do you mean by that?"

"Like you, I'm guessing."

"Ah, you see me as a threat? A danger?"

His eyes widened as she watched her hands slowly dropping to her waist, where they remained, gripping her sides, causing the slip to hitch up slightly, revealing more of those long, slim legs.

"No, not a danger. But something must have happened to force Simms to arrest you. Something bad."

"There's no proof." She turned and leaned against the bars. With the fingers of her left hand, she played with the ends of her hair. From this angle, Martinson had a clear sight of her breasts, the dark smudge of the nipples clearly visible.

"Well, I guess that's what Simms will bring."

"If he brings anything at all."

"I know him well enough to say nothing will stop him. No Indians, no robbers."

"A woman perhaps? A good woman could make him forget his duty."

"He has only recently lost his wife. And child."

"Ah, that's sad. I didn't know. And you? Are you married?"

She turned her face to him again and her eyes seemed like deep, inviting pools, so warm, so enticing that he could not look away. "No."

"You must long for the comfort of a woman, especially out here, in the hard, lonely plains of this desolate land."

The throbbing in his throat made it almost impossible to speak, and all he could manage was a strangulated, "Yes."

"Then why not come on in here and let's keep one another warm for a little while."

And before the words left her lips, she was already stepping back from the bars, her hands slowly moving to the shoulder straps of her slip to ease them down over her shoulders to expose her breasts. As the thin garment floated to her ankles, Martinson groaned, feasting on her body and, with all sensible thought cast aside, he fumbled for the keys and stumbled across to the cell, his desperation to consume her obvious in the growing bulge at his crotch.

"My, you are an eager boy," she said as the key rattled in the lock and Martinson pushed open the door. He fell into her, her arms wrapping around him to grip his buttocks as their lips melded together. "Slow," she breathed down his ear, her hand closing around his hardness, fingers finding the buttons of his trousers as his moans grew ever louder. "Oh yes, you are so lovely," she sighed as her hand found him and brought him out into the cold air.

In a whirl of desire, he did not notice her other hand until it was too late. With a yelp of frustration, he could only look in disbelief as she stepped away from him. In her left hand, she held his revolver, deftly lifted from its holster. And as he gaped, she drew back the hammer and her smile broadened. "So very lovely, and so very much like a man. Step away from the door."

She motioned with the gun and Martinson, as if in a dream, did as he was bid, hands coming up as if of their own volition. "Please," he said, voice tiny and frightened.

"Shut up with the whimpering," she snapped, waving the gun to the bunk. "Lie down on there." Her eyes narrowed. "I'll kill you if you don't."

He padded over, downcast, defeated, and flopped down. She stepped away and struggled to pull her slip back over her body.

"Simms will kill me when he finds out what happened," said Martinson and put his face in his hands. "Oh dear God. Dear God help me."

"Shut up, you simpleton. And put away that pathetic worm dangling there between your legs. Whatever made you think I could have anything to do with someone like you?"

"Oh please," he wailed, "please just go and leave me here. Please."

"Jesus," she breathed and put down the revolver as she took up the rest of her clothes and struggled into coarse, buckskin trousers, cotton overshirt and padded jacket. Martinson's muffled weeping accompanied every one of her movements. Shaking her head when finished, she released a mocking cackle. "It's a wonder to me how you survive out here, you weasel. I've a good mind to shoot you right now and put an end to your miserable life."

"I'm weak," he said, "weak and stupid. I'm so sorry."

"Pathetic," she said and reached for the gun just as the main door fell open.

A man stood silhouetted in the doorway, a tall, slim figure with long, braided hair and, although his features were obscured, Martinson recognised him at once. "Deep Water," he breathed.

Annabelle groaned as the man stepped up close, the carbine in his hands pointing unerringly towards her.

"Don't do anything stupid, ma'am," said the Indian, winking. "I've been listening at the door for quite a while, so why not just sit yourself right back down and you," he nodded to Martinson, "hitch up your pants and finish making that coffee."

Thirty five

They camped amongst a cluster of high, jagged rocks sprouting like giant's teeth from the surrounding snow-covered plains. Here, with the air a degree or so warmer, the ground was clear and Simms managed to make a fire, using his flint and steel to set alight a collection of coarse, dry grass and twigs. As it burnt he stacked on larger pieces of timber until the flames roared and they both huddled closer to bask in the glow.

"You're good," said Tabatha, drawing close to him. He draped his arm around her and held her close.

"I'm sorry," he mumbled.

"You must stop thinking about it," she said and pressed her mouth into his neck and kissed him. "It'll be just fine, you see."

He craned his neck, "What do you mean?"

"I mean, in time, we'll be able to be intimate without guilt."

His mouth dropped. "You mean—"

"I mean, we give it time."

He sat without answering, letting her words sink ever deeper. Words which bathed him in a warmth far greater than that of the fire. She understood, she accepted his dilemma, and it was wonderful to know. As the fire spluttered and crackled, he let his cheek to fall on top of her head and they sat and allowed that perfect moment to embrace them both.

Sometime in the night, he felt her move next to him, bringing her own blanket to join his. He did not move away as her young body snuggled into his back. The cold retreated as her hand moved over him and he stirred under her fingers.

"God, Tabatha," he breathed.

"Call me Tabby," she said.

He rolled over to face her. "Tabby," he whispered as his hands roamed over her body. They kissed and, cocooned in their embrace, they moved together and made long, slow love.

With the sun barely above the horizon, she found him squatting on top of one of the rocks, looking out across the plain. He did not flinch as she dropped down next to him, head on his shoulder. "Are you all right," she asked, her voice tinged with uncertainty.

At first he did not answer. When during those long hours ago, he lay spent in her arms, she kissed him tenderly on the throat, running her hands through his hair and he wept. She did not speak, but held him and he drifted off to sleep as if swathed in a soft eiderdown. Now, sitting here with her, he did not know what to say.

"It was lovely," she said. "You were lovely. I know you must feel – I don't know, perhaps awkward, a little embarrassed, but you don't need to be. It was meant to happen."

A smile flitted around at the corners of his mouth and he reached out and stroked her hair. "I don't think I've ever felt anything like this."

Now it was her turn to smile, her cheeks reddening slightly. "Me neither. When this is all over, perhaps we could spend some time together. Would you like that?"

"Very much."

She cupped her hand around his neck and drew him close. "I feel your hurt and I want it to go away. I can make it go away, if you'll let me."

"But why would you—"

She put her finger over his lips, "Don't. Just accept it."

They kissed and the feel of her smooth lips took all of his fears away. And all of his doubts. And questions.

But, as they rode out towards the town of Bovey, one question continued to niggle away. Some of the things Curly had said when they first met. Something which only now came back to place a tiny sense of unease inside Simms's gut. He'd been a deputy back in Kansas, the young man told him; he knew about the Pinkerton's jurisdiction, and he'd called Lamont 'Pa'. Yet he'd mentioned none of these things again when Simms put him forward as sheriff of Glory. As for Annabelle, Curly had forcibly denied she was his mother. Questions. Doubts. Miscalculations.

He shuddered.

"What are you thinking?" she asked, leaning across to grip his hand.

"How happy I am," he said and smiled to her.

And she smiled back, an open, warm, trusting smile, which drove the cold away and brought with it memories of the night before. So he put his worries aside and set his sights on Bovey looming ahead, a little under an hour away.

Thirty six

Pulling the flat-bottomed wagon to a halt on the outskirts of Glory, Shelby took out his pouch of tobacco and rolled himself a cigarette. As he took in the smoke, his eyes scanned the deserted main street and that instinctive sense for the unusual that he possessed forced him to turn his eyes to several of the building tops.

He spotted the first figure within a few seconds, huddled in a thick black coat, the barrel of a musket poking skywards. Perhaps it was too early for the sentry to notice Shelby's approach. Perhaps he was asleep, or even frozen to death. Stupid to be so exposed.

Roaming across to the opposite side, just next door to the Golden Nugget, another man with another firearm. Shelby released a long stream of smoke. So, here it was. The final confrontation. He wondered what had promoted the town to resort to these defensive measures. And Josh. Why had he done nothing to stop them? Was his wound still mortal, had he succumbed? And what of Stella? Had she not spoken of her love for him, or was that wishful thinking? Truth be known, he could not remember her exact words, but he wanted them to be of love and devotion. A woman like that, with all this money – he turned in his seat to check the saddlebags still lay where he had put them and grinned when he counted up the total, as he had any number of times since leaving that dreadful cabin of death. Of course, if Stella did not wish to take up the offer, there was always Mary. In many ways, she could prove the better option. For one thing, she wasn't a whore, eaten away by avarice. He chuckled at the idea.

He jumped down, stamped his feet several times to bring back some semblance of feeling, then tied up the old nag to a nearby post. Taking the saddlebags, he checked the sentries again. They remained in the same attitudes.

Neither had stirred. Draping the bags over his shoulder, he crossed the street and stepped up onto the boardwalk. Under the porch of an ironmonger's store he checked again for any movement from the man crouched on the rooftop across the street. Satisfied, he pressed down on the handle of the shop door and pushed it open.

Inside, the dim, miserable surroundings spoke of months, perhaps years of neglect. With its best times long behind it, the interior groaned under the weight of rusted implements hanging from the ceiling and adorning the walls, many of them covered with cobwebs and layers of dust. Cast-iron bath tubs and metal pails struggled for space with spades, picks, hoes and axes. A myriad of hopes and dreams, of planned new lives in the lands of the frontier, now abandoned amongst this plethora of rotting, unwanted wares. Shelby took a final draw on his cigarette and threw it down in disgust. The petty desires of nameless, disillusioned people. He hated them.

He eased his way behind the old, filthy counter and stepped into the back room. There was nothing here which spoke of habitation, just more metal tools and unopened boxes. Ignoring the door to his left, which he assumed led to the living area above the shop, he instead went through a door to the rear.

Finding himself in an alleyway, shielded from the main street, he pulled out his revolver and made his way down towards the back entrance of the Golden Nugget saloon. He could have shot the two sentries with ease, but such an action would remove the element of surprise. He wanted to keep that. He wanted to see the looks on the faces of what remained of the town council. They would be there, waiting. He knew it. He could sense it.

The rear room of the Golden Nugget appeared much the same as the ironmonger's had. Old discarded crates stacked in the corners, bits of furniture heaped up here and there, dozens of empty bottles strewn across the floor forcing him to tiptoe amongst them and find a pathway to the entrance into the bar area of the saloon.

Careful not to make too much noise, he eased open the door and looked into the bar. Empty of all customers, he strode to the staircase and ascended, taking each step with patient slowness, mindful of any creaks and groans. At the top, he took one more look to the bar below. Satisfied, he moved down the hallway to the door, which he knew led to where Josh rested. Placing his hand on the handle, he paused, not knowing if he would find his old partner alive, dead or still recovering. Whatever he found, Shelby had long since stopped caring. With the money, Stella or perhaps Mrs Hubert, life would be good here in Glory. Smiling, he let the saddlebags slip to the floor and went through into the bedroom.

They were both there, in bed, naked, Stella's limbs entwined with Josh's own. Both were asleep. For a moment, Shelby doubted the evidence of his eyes. He blinked several times, his stomach churning, all of his fanciful ideas vanishing in that single, awful moment. Yes, she was a whore, but he hoped their own coupling brought with it some hint of affection. He'd known many women, most of them whores. Affection was not something he knew much about, but this one seemed to promise so much. And now, here they were. The two of them. The ones he hoped to entrust with his schemes to take over this town, live the life of a gentleman, an owner of property, a man of means.

A cloud of despair settled over him. He'd suspected, of course, seen the way Stella looked at his friend, but he never allowed such thoughts to get in the way of his schemes. Now everything lay torn and tattered. Well, perhaps not everything. There was always Mrs Hubert. He stood and he gazed at them for a long time before coughing loud enough to cause Stella to stir and roll over.

Rubbing her eyes, she turned and faced Shelby. The look of complete disbelief overtaking her features almost sent him into a spasm of laughter, but anger overcame every other emotion. He raised his gun. As her mouth opened to scream, the hands imploring him, the head shaking, he shot her full in the face.

The great boom of the revolver brought everything to life in a sudden burst of activity. Josh scrambled out from under her destroyed, bloodied body. Shelby noted the bandages wrapped around his partner's midriff. Freshly applied, the dressing white and neat and clean. Josh's wound appeared almost healed, so Shelby shot him in the guts for good measure, enjoying the effect.

Squealing high-pitched as a pig, Josh writhed on the floor and Shelby stepped over him, crossing to the window to peer out to the rooftops opposite. From this angle, he had a reasonable view and saw the man standing up from his position, looking left and right. Shelby doubted he could shoot him from this distance, so he leaned out of the window and strained to look over to his left. The bedroom, positioned on the right side of the saloon, did not afford him a perfect view of the entrance so, annoyed, he stepped back into the room and went out, leaving Josh gasping and bleeding.

Shelby considered taking the saddlebags with him but decided they would slow him down, so he kicked them back inside the bedroom. They were heavy and he grunted with the effort. A door further down the hallway opened and a man came out, stuffing his shirt into his pants, hair tousled, clearly having only just woken up. He saw Shelby and the colour drained from his face.

"Well, if it isn't our good mayor, Mr Howard. How you doin', Mr Howard? Happy to see me?"

"Oh good God Almighty." Howard looked around in the desperate hope of finding an escape route.

"Didn't expect to see me so early in the morning, huh?" Shelby chuckled and moved down the hallway towards the babbling, quaking mayor. "Been enjoying yourself?" Now next to him, Shelby leaned his head around the door and caught sight of a young girl stepping out of the bed to gather up her clothes. Shelby chuckled again. "My, my, I never thought you had it in you."

"Listen, Shelby, for God's sake, we never thought you'd—"

"Save it," snapped Shelby. "Where's Springer? And Mrs Hubert, where might she be?"

"Home, I guess."

"Well, go and fetch them both. I need to call another meeting. Oh, and tell those two idiots outside to throw away their rifles before I put a hole in them big enough to ride a stagecoach through."

Thirty seven

Few people were out and about so early in the morning and the sound of the two horses' hooves scuffing over the snow-dusted street sounded too loud, bringing a feeling of foreboding to Simms as he reined in and dismounted.

"This is your town?" asked Tabatha, sliding down from her saddle. "Seems like it's dead."

"Just early," said Simms, tying his horse to the hitching rail outside his office. "I'm going to check in here before we go to the jailhouse."

"This is where you do all your work?" Tabatha stepped up onto the boardwalk and read the simple, wooden sign across the door. " 'Pinkerton Detective Agency. Agent Simms'. You're something of a celebrity, having your name written up here for everyone to see."

"Hardly a celebrity," he said with a grin as he fitted the key into the lock and turned it.

As usual, the cold bareness of the single room struck him as unwelcoming; he could not dismiss the memory of drinking himself into unconsciousness a mere handful of days ago. He turned to his desk and picked up the pieces of paper there. Telegrams. He scanned them and a cold chill ran through him.

"You have the keys to the jailhouse?"

He lowered his head, knowing the time had come. Heavy of heart he turned and looked at her, his own Navy Colt in her hand.

"You didn't really think I was going to help you, did you?"

She looked different now, her eyes hard, unfeeling, her mouth nothing but a thin, cruel line. Where had that soft, giving young woman gone, the one he loved with everything he had? Had she not moaned underneath him, held him so close he believed she would crush the breath out of him? Simms allowed his shoulders to drop. "I thought we had something."

"You were wrong, Detective. How could you seriously believe I would ever want to be with someone like you, although I must say you were mighty fine." She chuckled and eased back the hammer of the Colt. "I'm going down to the jailhouse and setting Ma free, then we'll ride back to get Curly. That was a bad move setting Curly up as sheriff in that God-awful place. You have no idea who he is."

Simms, his eyes clouding over with a heavy sadness, shook his head and picked up one of the telegram messages. "I do now. Seems like you didn't leave Kansas for the reasons you said. "

"How the hell would you know that?"

"Because I asked a good friend of mine to send a message across to Fort Bridger, see if there was a warrant out for you and that bastard Lamont."

"You be careful what you say, Detective." She clamped her teeth together in a snarl. "I will shoot you right now, if I have a mind to."

"Yes, I do believe you would." He placed the telegram back onto his desk. "Curly is a wanted man. Seems he shot and killed his last employer then helped himself to a stash of money."

"Sheriff Coltrane was a loathsome swine. He treated Curly like a piece of shit."

"So, he deserved to die?" She nodded. "So why did you fall in with Lamont?"

"He was fixing on leaving, just as he told you. So, we hitched along, seeing as he and Ma were as good as wed."

"So you really are with Curly."

Her smile broadened. "He's the finest man I've ever known."

"You didn't say so last night, nor this morning."

"I'm a good actress."

"Did last night mean nothing to you at all?"

Another mocking snigger. "Well, a little. I enjoyed it, if that's what you mean, but I'll soon forget it. Ain't no one can hold a candle to Curly."

"Well, in a weird kind of way, that makes what happens next a lot easier."

A frown creased her lovely face. "What in hell does that mean?"

"It means I took the lead out from that Navy you're holding whilst you were sleeping last night. All you got is a chamber full of powder."

She gaped at him before her eyes dropped to the gun in disbelief. In one bound, he crossed the room. She squeezed the trigger and the powder flashed, but nothing but a cloud of smoke followed and Simms wrenched the gun from her numbed fingers before backhanding her to the ground.

"I should kill you," he said through gritted teeth. "Instead, you'll rot in jail, just like Curly's mother."

"Curly will kill you," she whimpered, looking up at him through eyes thick with tears. "He'll kill you and come back for us."

"The hell he will," he said, gripping her by the collar, hauling her to her feet. He pressed his face close. "A good actor, you say? Well not as goddamned good as me."

"You liar. You wanted me."

"I *used* you. And you were a damn sight cheaper than a whore."

"*Liar!*" She struggled in his grip, but it was useless. The fight went out of her and she surrendered to him as he dragged her out of the office towards the jailhouse.

Miller screwed up his mouth as he read through the three telegrams, then waved them towards Martinson. "Why the hell didn't you show me these before?"

Martinson shrugged, "What's an ignorant storekeeper supposed to do in the face of such officialdom?"

Miller frowned and Simms quickly stepped in, taking the messages out of Miller's fist. "I think what he means is he wanted to see the look on your face as I stood here and watched you read them."

"Did he, by God?"

Martinson beamed and leaned back in his chair. "So what do we do now?"

Simms looked across to the cell and the two women sitting inside on the simple bed, heads down, silent as stone. "I'm going back to Glory and bring in Curly."

"You need help?" asked Miller.

Simms shook his head. "I already got some."

He doffed his hat and stepped outside. As his hand pulled on the door to close it, Martinson appeared, a sheepish look crossing his face. "I need to tell you something."

Simms looked at him. "I'll meet Deep Water a little ways out of town."

"I thought as much. That's why I need to talk to you. I let you down, Detective. If it hadn't been for Deep Water, that Annabelle woman would have got away."

"Oh? And why is that?"

"She – she sort of took advantage of me. Like a fool, I couldn't resist and if Deep Water hadn't burst in when he did ..."

Simms smiled and clamped his hand on his friend's shoulder. "We're men; we're weak when it comes to a beautiful woman. I should know, old friend."

"You mean Noreen? But Noreen was—"

"No, not Noreen." He let out a long breath and turned his gaze to the street. By now, townspeople were moving from building to building, riders came and went, carriages clattered by. Every so often, a passerby would wave or call out a greeting. Simms watched it all without comment. "I'll tell you about it one day. Until then, don't bust yourself up over succumbing to her charms. Nothing happened. She's still behind bars and she'll answer for what she did. Tabatha too."

"And the other one – Curly?"

"I aim to bring him in, like I said. You, you get yourself back to your store and perhaps call into my place if you could. Set a fire, air it through. The snow might have passed, but the cold still grips hard. Will you do that for me?"

"You know I will."

Simms squeezed the man's shoulder again, then stepped down towards his horse and prepared to ride out of town to Glory.

Thirty eight

Shelby positioned himself behind the bar, a glass of beer on the counter, the sawn-off shotgun usually kept out of view, lying in front of him. His stomach rumbled with hunger but he decided to eat after the meeting with the town council. So he drank his beer and waited. A smile crossed his face, a smile of satisfaction at his own cunning. If all went as planned, within a very short time he would have the whole town under his control and the money would roll in.

When the swing doors opened, however, it wasn't Springer who came in, but a thin, gaunt looking individual with a mop of red hair, a snub nose and bucked teeth. Shelby thought he recognised him and was about to speak when two others entered and took up position behind him, carbines cradled in their arms.

"We're here to arrest you," said the snub-nosed redhead.

"You're here to do *what*?"

"We're sworn deputies and we're here to bring you in. You can either come easy or we'll take you by force."

"Now ain't that just dandy." Shelby grinned and took another drink. He was about to lower the glass when he froze. From out of the corner of his eye, he spotted yet another man stepping into the bar through the back door. But this one seemed different. The look on his face was one Shelby had seen many times before. With extreme care, Shelby lowered the glass.

"It's your play," said this stranger.

"And who in the hell are you?"

"I'm the sheriff. Keep your hand well away from that shotgun or I'll shoot you where you stand."

Shelby arched a single eyebrow and took a moment to consider his options. "Well, that says all that needs saying. Sheriff? Seems like things have changed somewhat since I was last here."

"Yes they have."

The sheriff appeared relaxed, his hands hanging heavy, frock coat pulled back to reveal a holstered Remington at his side.

"All right," said Shelby. He nodded towards the redhead. "You boys take it easy. I'll just finish my beer then I'll be right with you."

He reached over for the glass and saw the redhead move to his own revolver. Fate played its hand, as it always did, the moment decided. In a blur, Shelby swept up the shotgun and discharged both barrels towards the three men in the doorway before he dived to the floor just as the sheriff loosed off two rounds to slap into the bar counter, sending up a spray of wooden shards and smashed glass.

Rolling over onto his back, Shelby lay still, mouth open, breathing controlled. He brought out the revolver from his belt and slowly shuffled backwards, barrel aimed towards the far end of the bar. From somewhere close he heard the moans of the wounded. His hope was the shotgun blast had at least disabled the three at the main door and, from what he heard, he believed this to be the case. As he reached the corner of the counter, he turned on his side and chanced a quick look.

They were on their backs. The redhead was clearly dead, having received most of the blast. His comrades were writhing, the man closest in the worst state, his chest a perforated bloody mess. The third man, on the far side, was struggling to sit up. Shelby calmly took a bead on the man's head and blew it apart with his revolver.

From near the rear of the bar, the sheriff's voice shouted out, "I'll kill you, you bastard!"

Gauging the distance and the direction of the voice, Shelby drew in a breath and reared up from his cover.

The sheriff, a man to whom gunfights were something he must have been involved in many times, had set himself up in the corner behind an upturned table. Shelby, panicking when he could not detect the man's hiding place, fired off three more quick blasts before the sheriff returned fire and hit him high up on the left shoulder, throwing him backwards into a stash of crated up bottles and other glassware, his gun clattering away from his grip with the impact of the fall. He lay there, the breath knocked out of him, pain lancing through the wound. He took a glance towards his gun and, as he did so, a pair of booted feet loomed into his field of vision.

"You filthy sonofabitch," said the sheriff, kicking the gun out of reach. "I've a good mind to blow your brains out right here right now. But I'll save it for this afternoon, when you'll hang in main street, in front of everyone."

"You can't do that," muttered Shelby, broken and defeated amongst the shattered glass. He coughed, hawked and spat. "This is my town, you bastard."

"I'll put a notice around your neck to that effect," said the sheriff with a grin.

The bat-winged doors creaked open and Shelby craned his neck to see Mrs Hubert stepping inside. She took a quick glance around the scene of carnage and then, with her hand pressed to her mouth, turned her gaze to Shelby. "Oh my God," she managed.

"It's all done, Mrs Hubert," said the sheriff, stepping away. "This murdering heap of shit will be swinging by a rope come this evening."

Stooping down, Mrs Hubert picked up Shelby's gun and appeared to inspect it with great care. "Strange how things have a way of playing themselves out," she said as she raised the gun and fired.

Thirty nine

Coming into Glory on that last, cold, frosty morning, Simms stopped at the far end of the main street and peered towards the Golden Nugget. There were two horses hitched outside together with a flat-bottomed wagon, but other than these there were no signs of life. Certainly not from the body hanging from a telegraph pole close by. Simms kicked his horse's flanks and moved closer. Strung up to the wooden shaft, the body rigid, with its face twisted and the flesh already black from dried blood and the intense cold, it must have been there for some time. Simms leaned forward in his saddle to read the notice around the corpse's neck. 'This man tried to take our town. He failed.'

Then he looked up to the face again and sighed.

"Seems like my work's been done for me," he said aloud and turned to move across to the saloon, leaving Curly's body dangling behind him.

A fire crackled in the grate and a barman was polishing the counter as Simms pushed open the doors and stepped inside. He nodded to the barman's perplexed look and went across to the flames, pulling off his gloves and warming his hands.

"We're not open," came a voice.

Simms looked over his shoulder. "Just getting warm. I've a mind to visit the mayor. You know where he is?"

The barman produced a sawn-off shotgun from underneath counter. "I said we're not open."

Taking a deep breath, Simms pressed his lips together and turned. "If you don't mind me saying, you're a mite unfriendly."

"I'll be a darn sight more unfriendly if you don't get the hell out." To give emphasis to his words, he eased back both hammers.

Simms cocked his head. "You know, at this distance, which must be all of twenty feet, I doubt you can hit me with that thing. But this," Simms drew back his coat and tapped the handle of his Colt Dragoon, "this will blow off your fucking head with ease, so just put down the goddamned gun and tell me where the mayor is."

With a deal of reluctance, the barman placed the shotgun back on the counter top. "The mayor is dead."

A tiny tremor of alarm coursed through Simms. "And Mr Springer?"

"He's at home, I reckon. Who in the hell are you?"

"I could ask the same of you."

"My name is Morris. I'm a deputy, just helping out around here. We had something of an incident in here yesterday."

"A deputy? So what in the hell is the sheriff doing strung up outside like a prize turkey?"

"Is that you, Detective?"

Simms looked up to the top of the stairs to see Mrs Hubert slowly making her way down. She was dressed in a silk dressing gown of deep blue and, as she descended, her bare legs slipped out from between the folds of the material, causing Simms to consider whether she was naked underneath. "Good morning, Mrs Hubert," said Simms, trying to maintain his composure.

"I'll deal with this," she said towards Morris, dismissing him with a wave of the hand.

As she approached, the waft of her perfume reached Simms's nostrils. He studied her with much appreciation. "Things have certainly changed around here, Mrs Hubert."

"Yes. For the better, I believe." She was within a step away now. "I must say, your return was not expected."

"Oh? And why is that?"

"From what our good sheriff told me the day before he died."

"You mean the plans he made with Tabatha? Well, plans unravel."

"Don't they just." She put her hands on her hips. "You're a survivor, Detective. Like me. We do what is necessary."

"It seems that way. What happened to Curly?"

"He got in the way."

Nodding, Simms glanced upstairs. "The kid up there, the wounded one? What about him?"

"Dead, sorry to say. Stella also. Howard. Every one of them who stood against us."

"Us? You mean you and Springer?"

Her face erupted into laughter. "Dear God, Detective, don't be such a damned fool. You expect a woman like me to fall in with a slime like Springer? No, no, he's nothing but a puppet, a purveyor of money. He does my bidding now that I'm in charge. Well," she gestured up stairs, "I can't take all the credit. I have my partner."

"I see."

"Do you? I'm not at all sure if you do. We're going to make something of this town, Detective, put it back on the map. I have contacts back East. Magazine and newspaper editors, investment bankers. We're going to advertise this town as a good place to live, one where families can settle, safe and secure. The nearby mines will reopen and soon the money will come rolling in."

"You'll need a lot of money to develop this place."

"I have lots of money, Detective."

"And Curly? Stella, the boy, Howard? You think you can simply put their murders down to expenses?"

"Collateral damage, Detective. Nothing more, nothing less. They got in the way. I won't allow that."

Simms pulled in a breath. "You seem to forget there will be a U.S. Marshal arriving before long, now the snow is finally receding. Once he gets here, he'll want answers."

"And he'll get them."

"You've changed your tune, Mrs Hubert. From what I recall, you were a woman of virtue, one who respected the law, who—"

"You sound like a preacher, Detective, and I don't like being preached to. I woke up, truth be told. Woke up to the possibilities. Since my husband's death, I've lived an empty life, no dreams, no hope for the future. When the opportunity arose, I grabbed it and I'm not about to let it go."

"People have died. Someone has to answer for that."

Her expression grew hard. "Well, I don't have to answer to you. You're nothing here, Detective."

"I'm the law and from where I'm standing that's something this town is in sore need of."

A gruff voice shouted across the room, "Get out, you sanctimonious bastard, before we take you out."

As if this were the signal, Morris came from around the bar, the shotgun in his hands. From the other direction another man, the owner of the voice, revolver in hand, smiling, stepped through the door at the foot of the stairs. Both these men sported stars on their vests.

"I really would advise you to leave," said Mrs Hubert.

Simms took his time, looking past Mrs Hubert to the top of the stairs and a third man, bare-chested, left shoulder heavily bandaged, leaning against the balustrade. "Who's this?"

"His name is Simms," said Mrs Hubert. "He's a Pinkerton detective. He's here to serve justice."

"Is he, by God?" He made his way slowly down the stairs.

Simms noted the revolver stuck in his waistband. Three armed men and Mrs Hubert. Simms shook his head. "I'll take your advice," he said and smiled. "The Marshal can deal with this."

"Very wise, Detective," said Mrs Hubert. "No hard feelings."

"None at all."

Doffing his hat, he strolled over to the door, aware of the eyes boring into his back, and stepped outside into the cold, sharp morning air.

A man was ambling from across the street. Simms recognised him as the old timer who greeted him the first time he rode into Glory. Anguish played around every line in his aged face. As he drew closer, Simms cast a quick glance towards the double-swing doors.

"Mister, I think you'd better get over to the bank. Right now."

Simms went to his horse and pulled out his carbine from its sheath. He checked it and nodded to the old man, whose lips were trembling. Indeed, on closer examination, Simms noted every fibre of his ancient frame was quaking. "What in the hell is wrong?"

"Mr Springer. They shot him and left him in there, sitting behind his desk with a hole as big as a melon in his head, not there is much left of his head. And the money. All the money is gone. You gotta come and take a look, because I'm not sure if—"

"Is the telegraph fixed yet?"

Dempsey's eyes bulged. "What in tootin' hell are you thinking of—"

"Is it fixed?"

"I ain't sure."

"Well, you get the hell over there and send a message to Bridger. You think you can remember?"

"I'm not an idiot, mister. I can remember stuff."

"Good. In that case, get a message off to Bridger and tell them to make sure the Marshal is coming and that he ain't coming alone. Then you find yourself some cover, you hear?"

The old man nodded and blustered away back across the street. Simms looked opposite to the roof of the building and took a breath.

The saloon doors creaked open and Simms responded to the heavy tread of boots on floorboards. Keeping the horse between him and the entrance, he leaned across his saddle and eyed the two men standing there.

"We told you to get the hell out," said the first one, the barman, still sporting the shotgun.

"Seems I changed my mind."

The words sparked the men into action. As they moved, Simms brought up his carbine and shot the barman through the throat just as a second bullet whistled past his ear and hit the other deputy in the chest, blasting him backwards through the double swing doors.

Simms dropped the carbine and drew the Dragoon, stopping only briefly to give a look and a salute towards the roof opposite. From his position Deep Water raised his hand and then dropped out of sight again.

A stifled yelp forced Simms to swing around.

Dempsey, his old, tired legs not able to take him across to the telegraph office quick enough, struggled and whimpered whilst the man with the injured shoulder held him around the throat. Simms groaned, realising the man must have come out of the saloon's back entrance. He holstered his gun and strode out into the middle of the street.

"Let him go," said the detective, bringing his hands up. "This has nothing to do with him. Just you and me."

The wounded man's eyes twinkled and he gnawed away at his bottom lip as he considered the invitation. Dempsey wriggled, gasping for breath, and the man dropped him. Not waiting for a second chance, Dempsey scrambled to his feet and teetered away. The man grinned and brought up his arm to shoot the old-timer where he stood.

It was all the time Simms needed.

His hand came up from his holster, the big Dragoon loosing three evenly placed shots, hitting the man in the chest, the heavy lead slugs blowing his body apart, sending him crashing to the ground.

From his position across the street, Dempsey took up a terrible wailing as Simms walked over to what was left of the wounded man's body. Within two paces, a woman's voice cut through the cold air. Simms turned to see Mrs Hubert stood in the doorway, face aghast. "Shelby! Oh dear God, *Shelby*!"

She came across the street at a wild run, dressing gown gaping open, the gun in her hand blazing. Simms whirled and crouched low. The shots were ill-aimed, sporadic, and as she ran she stumbled, tripped and fell.

"Oh Shelby," she whimpered, palms down in the ground, hair falling down to form a sort of veil. Her sobs shuddered through her body, filling the still and silent street with their mournful sound.

With the tears streaming down her cheeks, she brought up her face, put the barrel into her mouth and put the last remaining bullet through her brain.

Forty

For three days, Simms waited at Glory. He set up an interim headquarters at the sheriff's office, sending Deep Water back to Bovey to inform Miller what had transpired. He had gathered affidavits from those willing to come forward and sent these with the scout. Now, in the dreary office, with Old Man Dempsey flitting in and out to ensure all was as well as expected; the persons from whom he gleaned any further details were the town doctor and the telegraph operator. Both men were skittish initially, not sure of the situation and fearful of reprisals. As the days passed, however, it became clear that any allies Shelby once had were now either dead or had changed sides. A wave of relief washed over the town and a new sense of optimism developed. Sitting on the veranda, watching the townsfolk drift by, Simms noted their cheery demeanours and the way they greeted him, their saviour. A town not unlike Bovey, he mused. Perhaps a little more downtrodden, but with an equal measure of potential. All it needed was someone with the right leadership skills, someone with a vision.

"I'm not really the sort of man you're looking for, Detective," said Doctor Grove during their first meeting together on the morning after Shelby's death. "I didn't sit on the town council and have no real experience of procedures or legal wrangling."

"You didn't sit on the council because you weren't part of their clique," said Simms. "Springer held sway over them all."

"That's true," interjected Cooper, the telegraph operator. "Nothing much changed until Shelby turned up. Even Forbes simply fitted in."

"I'm curious about him," said Simms. "Why would the council accept him as sheriff without making proper checks? All it would need was a message to Laramie to find out if there were any charges hanging over him."

"Isn't it obvious?" said Grove. "He was in cahoots with Springer from the start. But when Judge Malpas confronted them, things began to unravel. I suppose they thought by killing him they would have a clear run."

"Until someone sent a telegram requesting a marshal." Simms held the doctor's stare. "I'm guessing that was you?"

Grove nodded once and Simms sighed. "No doubt they had some plans for all that money, but God knows what."

The telegraph operator cleared his throat. "No doubt you have some such plans, Detective?"

Simms wrinkled his brow at Cooper's remark. "I'll take it back to Bridger and hand it over to the authorities. I'll be sending them a telegraph as soon as the line is back up."

"Should be by the end of this afternoon."

"It's stolen money and should go back to those who lost it," said Grove.

"I quite agree. I'll also send some messages back to my Headquarters in Illinois to ensure just that. When the Marshal arrives, things can begin to move forward in this town. Mr Grove, I really do think you should consider setting up as mayor. There isn't anyone else with your authority or standing in the town."

"I'll think about it. Talk to my wife."

"The first thing we need to do is think about appointing a sheriff."

"It's a pity that can't be you," said Cooper.

"I can't be two things at once. Besides, I have my office back at Bovey."

"Bovey is only a day's ride away," put in Grove. "If you have a mind to, you could combine both offices. It might be something worth considering. I'm not sure what your pay is as an agent for the Pinkertons but, if I'm elected, I'll make damn sure you get a good salary as sheriff."

Simms pursed his lips and sat back in his chair. "So … You think you will run for mayor?"

"I *think*," said Cooper with a smile, "that together, we could make a real go of this place."

And Simms stared without speaking as his mind ran through all the permutations.

* * *

The U.S Marshal who rode into Glory on the late afternoon of the third day was a tall, thin, surly looking gentleman of indeterminate age. Sporting long grey hair and a pointed beard, his small eyes stared with a penetrating intensity that many found unsettling. Accompanying him were three other equally stoic individuals, none of whom seemed particularly pleased with their current assignment. Simms, standing outside the sheriff's office, watched them dismount and tie up their horses.

"Name's Middleton," said the Marshal, stepping up next to the Pinkerton. "You'll be Simms presumably."

Stepping aside, Simms waved the Marshal into the confines of the office. The others waited outside, arranging themselves in a line, ever watchful.

"Got a message for you from Chicago."

Simms arched an eyebrow as Middleton handed over the folded paper. Simms read it and grunted. His headquarters wanted him to report to them, at his earliest convenience, with the money and a full report of what had happened.

"I need to go to Bovey and ensure the judge there has all the details of the case against those two women."

"Yes, I've been instructed to give you some information pertaining to that too." Middleton's eyes narrowed still further. "Seems as your chief witness is dead, there is no case to answer. Those women are free to go."

Simms's mouth fell open. "You've got to be kidding me?"

"Do I look as though I'm kidding?"

Speechless, Simms drifted around the desk and sank down into his chair with a heavy sigh. "But I saw it, saw the whole damned thing."

"It's your word against theirs, I'm afraid to say. No one is doubting you, Detective, but without corroborative evidence delivered by witnesses, there is no chance of a conviction. The most you could get the second one for is attempted murder, if anyone will come forward to confirm she did indeed discharge her firearm at you."

"You know a lot."

"I know the whole damn case, Detective. Circuit judge works close with us on all such prosecutions. I'm sorry, but it's all been for nothing."

"So they go free?"

"They're already free, Detective. By the time you get back to Bovey they'll be long gone." The Marshal took in a deep breath. "Now, perhaps we can set our minds on establishing some order in this town by electing a mayor and appointing a sheriff. Any thoughts?"

"Plenty."

"Let's hear them."

And Simms told him of Cooper's suggestion. Middleton pulled up a chair and listened as he carefully filled a bone pipe with tobacco. He puffed away and, after some reflection, finally grunted, blowing out a long stream of smoke, "I think it's an admirable suggestion, one which I endorse fully." He grinned and leaned forward, putting out his hand. "Congratulations on your new appointment, Sheriff."

Forty one

Simms listened to what Sheriff Miller had to say. He'd rode into Bovey at the end of yet another blustery day, the wind whipping around like a thousand Ute arrows, attacking every inch of exposed flesh. His nose streamed and his jaw ached with the constant gritting of teeth. Time was always against him.

"I had no choice," explained Miller, pouring Simms a cup of coffee. "The order came through and the judge made the ruling."

"I should have been here."

"I doubt if there would be anything you could have done." Miller handed over a steaming cup and Simms, huddled in his overcoat and still wearing his scarf and gloves, nodded his thanks. Miller sank into his chair. "I know I was always dubious over that older woman, but the young one seemed like a firebrand to me. And she took a shot at you, despite the gun being unloaded. Seems strange that the judge did not take that into consideration."

"Seems strange to me too. I have a bad feeling about all of this."

"Well, there ain't nothing to be done about it now."

"I guess not. I'll go and take a look at my place, make sure it's all in order, then I have to make my way down to Bridger and return the money. Deep Water will accompany me."

"You put a lot of trust in that Indian. Martinson does too. I don't get it at all. They're all damned savages. Have you heard the news from Twin Buttes?"

"Twin Buttes? What's that?"

"A town, maybe three days north, on the far side of the River. A war party of Utes hit it a few days ago. Never heard of such a thing."

"They must be desperate."

"Well, desperate or not, they killed a heap of people before the locals got together and made a stand. Seems like they had some help, but the details are still sketchy. Thing is," he leaned forward, his face growing dark and serious, "if them Indians are brave enough to attack a town, none of us are safe."

"I reckon once this weather breaks and spring kicks in, things will change. The Utes want to eat, just like any of us. But it's a dangerous development for sure. Listen, once I get to Bridger, I'll see if Johnstone can allow a troop to come over here, give us some support."

"I thought you would be taking up your office in Glory on your return?"

"I will, but I'm hoping to split my duties. It'll mean a lot more travelling than I hoped but, hell, it can't be helped. I need a regular job."

Miller grunted and stretched out his legs. "Being a sheriff of a small town ain't what it's cracked up to be, Simms. Most days I sit around scratching my head wondering what to do."

"Maybe I'll take a look at Twin Buttes."

"Might be worth investigating, in your other position as a Pinkerton. Who knows?" He grinned. "You don't let the grass under your feet, do you?"

"Don't see no use in just sitting around waiting for things to happen. No offence."

"None taken. This job suits me just dandy. The quiet, that's what I long for. Those two women, that's the nearest I've come to excitement since I took up this job."

"Yeah, well, they were mighty attractive."

"I didn't mean that sort of excitement, Simms."

"Yeah, I know. It was a joke."

Miller grunted and stood up. "Martinson left with those women, said he was going to sell them some munitions and—"

"Martinson left with them?" Simms stood up, coffee forgotten. "Why the hell didn't you tell me before?"

"There's no harm in it, for God's sake. Them two are innocent. You need to swallow that down, Detective, before you—"

"Them two *innocents* are meaner than a pack of wolves, Sheriff. Believe you me."

"I don't. And neither does the judge."

Simms whirled around and made for the door. "I'm going to check on Martinson. I hope to God you're right – and I'm wrong."

Miller went to say something but, before he could get a single word out, Simms was gone.

* * *

He covered the distance between the town and Martinson's place in rapid time, pushing his horse, already tired from the journey from Glory, to its limits. Some fifty or so paces from the Swede's merchant store, the horse staggered to a halt, blown. Simms reined it in, whispering soft words of encouragement into its ear, but the horse was beyond coaxing. Its breath steamed into the cold evening air, its flanks heaving. Mindful of its suffering, not wishing to put the creature's life in danger, Simms slid down from the saddle, stroked the horse's neck and drew out the sheathed carbine strapped to the side. He crossed the open plain towards the merchant store at a jog, alert, eyes watchful for any signs of movement. With each step, the surrounding light grew dimmer. A single, dreary candle burned in one of the shop front windows, almost set there as a beacon, drawing him closer. He slowed to a walk, reached the main door, squatted down and listened.

There were two windows either side of the door. He took a quick glance through the one to his right. The room was dark, with nothing visible inside. He recalled the layout of the building, remembering the darkened room must be the store, with the kitchen on the far side. Martinson's merchant store also served as an eating place, one at which travellers on their way West could stop over, rest and enjoy a good meal. Simms remembered his first visit, when he came in, asking for—

A piece of hot lead slapped into the woodwork next to him. He rolled away and took flight, zigzagging across the ground towards the side of the building. Another shot rang out, more ill-aimed than the first, and Simms threw himself out of sight, pressing himself against the wall.

The sound of scurrying feet forced him to chance a look. There was nothing but the open plain, the shadow of his distant horse the only living thing out there. Keeping low, he edged his way to the far end and saw her, bent double, running from the little barn across the way. She held a carbine in her hands and was making for the cover afforded by a small outhouse. Simms cursed. It seemed like Annabelle but the poor light made identifying her difficult and the possibility of a shot impossible. Biting down on his lip, he tried the side door and breathed a sigh as it swung open.

Inside, the small confines of the storeroom pressed in on him. It was too dark to walk through it without bashing into any number of utensils and boxes, so he waited, straining to hear anything from beyond the far door. A tiny sliver of light crept out from under the door at the far end. Not strong enough to see by, Simms slid down the wall and bided his time. If it was Annabelle outside, her intentions were clear. The same could be said for Tabatha, wherever she was. As for Martinson, he may already be dead and the thought fell over Simms like a heavy weight, pressing him down, forcing him to sink further into himself with the horror or it all.

As it was, fate acted for him. The door through which he had come burst open and the woman came in, her breath rasping, the carbine held out. "I'm going to kill you, Detective, then eat your damned liver."

In the darkness of that tiny room, the one discernible object was the open door, the shape of the woman silhouetted there against the dying strands of daylight. He didn't hesitate and put a shot from his carbine through her body.

Voices cried out from the other room. Two voices, one high-pitched and angry, the other as if from someone in pain. A door creaked open, pounding feet disappearing into the evening. Simms waited, controlling his breathing. He put the carbine down and pulled out the Dragoon, easing back the hammer before creeping forward on his knees. At the door, he stopped, looking back at the body of the woman, lying there, silent and still.

He strained to hear anything from the room beyond, but the only sound to reach him was the low moaning of someone who suffered. He pushed open the door and ducked back at once, expecting a further blast from another firearm.

Nothing happened. He waited. A tiny croak from somewhere within, uttered as a warning or perhaps a cry of despair. Unable to decide, Simms took a quick look and peered into the very bowels of hell itself.

He slumped back out of sight again, both hands clasping the Dragoon, face upturned, not daring to believe the sight waiting for him mere footsteps away.

"Martinson," whispered Simms after several seconds slipped by. "Martinson, is she there?"

A prolonged moan, followed by a wheezing, "No," and Simms knew it was safe to move inside.

Stretched along the shop counter, Martinson lay, hands and feet lashed down with thin cord, pulled so tight they bit into the flesh. Naked, hair, chest and nether regions shaved by a blunt razor or knife, body covered with a multitude of nicks and cuts. Heavy bruising spread across his ribs and lower abdomen, his mouth and nose caked in dried, black blood. As he turned his head to face Simms, the tears came, probably more from shame than pain and Simms, trying his best to appear encouraging, forced a smile and went up to his friend.

As he pulled out a knife from the sheath in his boot, the sound of pounding hooves receding into the distance forced him to curtail releasing his friend as he ran to the main door and tore it open. Bringing up his revolver, he already knew Tabatha was out of range, her body low over the neck of the horse, slapping its rump with her hand, driving it across the plain at a tremendous pace.

"Damn her to hell," spat Simms and let out a long, frustrated sigh. He went back to Martinson and cut through the restraining cords. Simms helped him to sit up, his old friend breaking down at that point, hanging onto Simms like a child with its parent, his sobs filling the room.

"I couldn't do anything," he said, voice quivering. "They told me they knew you would come. I wanted to try and do something, but when they held a knife to my throat and said ... "

"It's all right, Martinson. You don't have to explain."

"Yes, yes I do, because I feel..." A stifled moan came from the back of his throat as he fought to keep himself under control, his whole body shuddering with the effort. "They told me they were going to cut open my belly and pull out my innards. Like executioners of old, they said. Oh dear Christ, when they put me down and began to scrape off my hair, I thought – I thought I was in hell, Simms. Their eyes... they were like demons. And no matter how much I wanted, I couldn't – I couldn't do a damned thing."

"Martinson, anyone in your position would have—"

"They said they would kill you, but not before they cut out your heart and ate it right there, right in front of you." He broke down completely, unable to hold back his anguish any longer as his face crumpled.

Simms held him without speaking, knowing no words existed which would help Martinson come to terms with what had happened. And Simms wondered about that. Wondered about what might have happened, what their devilish plan was. He'd discover it all in time, but when that time might be, he had no idea. All he knew was that one day, he would meet Tabatha again to make sure she paid her dues. But when his mind turned to how their bodies had moved so deliciously together, how her hands held him, her back arched, her voice whispered his name, he couldn't help but feel the jarring, overwhelming sense of regret welling up inside him. How he'd strained to condemn her on their last meeting, how he'd lied when he told her he used her. He hung his head and held onto Martinson with all his might.

* * *

She rode on throughout the following day, putting distance behind her, keeping her mind free from concerns over Annabelle and how close she had come to death. Simms played her well, his performance so believable. She knew now she should have killed him the first opportunity she had, back in that old rickety hotel when she found him asleep.

Towards the end of the day, she dismounted and led her horse amongst an outcrop of rocks and trees, which for the most part were free from snow. She beat her arms around herself, desperate to bring life back to her frozen body. She climbed the highest rock and looked out towards the north. The river rolled through the plain, a silver streak in the whiteness of the land. If it were frozen, she might chance crossing it, but it would be risky. If she slipped and fell …

Beyond the river, on the far bank, however she made the crossing, she would strike out and reach the nearest town. She did not know if such a town existed, but felt sure there must be one. Wherever and whatever it was, she again would play her game, put on her angelic, innocent face and win over the hearts of those in charge. And when she was well set and had enough allies, she would seek out Simms once again.

And kill him.

THE END

Dear reader,

We hope you enjoyed reading *To Die in Glory*. Please take a moment to leave a review, even if it's a short one. Your opinion is important to us.

Discover more books by Stuart G. Yates at https://www.nextchapter.pub/authors/stuart-g-yates

Want to know when one of our books is free or discounted for Kindle? Join the newsletter at http://eepurl.com/bqqB3H

Best regards,

Stuart G. Yates and the Next Chapter Team

The story continues in:
A Reckoning by Stuart G. Yates

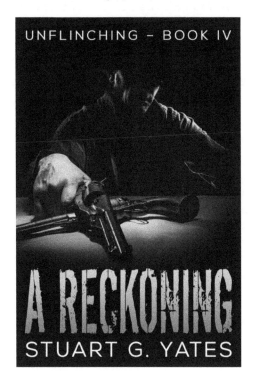

To read the first chapter for free, head to:
https://www.nextchapter.pub/books/a-reckoning

About the Author

Stuart G Yates is the author of a eclectic mix of books, ranging from historical fiction through to contemporary thrillers. Hailing from Merseyside, he now lives in southern Spain, where he teaches history, but dreams of living on a narrowboat in Shropshire.